"Tell me about Michael Young," he said. "How long was he missing before his body was found?"

"There wasn't . . . a body. Just clothing, and bones. I believe it was seven months altogether before berry-pickers discovered the remains, in a gully where he'd fallen."

"How was he identified? By dental charts?"

"No. I recognized the plaid coat he'd had on the night he disappeared. That seemed to be . . . . enough."

"He'd be about twenty-six today, wouldn't he?"

"Yes," Helen said.

"If he were alive . . . if Michael Young were alive after all, then some of our questions would be answered. . . ."

"Farris has marvelous skill."   —*Associated Press*

"His paragraphs are smashingly crafted and his images glitter like solitaires."
                          —*The Philadelphia Inquirer*

Tor books by John Farris

JOHN FARRIS

WHEN MICHAEL CALLS

TOR

A TOM DOHERTY ASSOCIATES BOOK
NEW YORK

WHEN MICHAEL CALLS

Copyright © 1967 by John Farris

Cover art by Dave Fishman

A Tor Book
Published by Tom Doherty Associates, Inc.
49 West 24th Street
New York, N.Y. 10010

ISBN: 0-812-50356-2

First Tor edition: November 1991

Printed in the United States of America

0 9 8 7 6 5 4 3 2 1

The yellow Shades County school bus dropped Peggy Connelly and two other second-graders off at the corner and Peggy walked the rest of the way atop the low stone wall that separated the Connelly property from the street, taking care not to scuff her good school shoes. A tall young man was digging in the front yard and Peggy paused for a few moments near the white gate in the wall. Peggy didn't particularly like Randle and avoided him whenever possible, but she couldn't resist a freshly dug hole, so she hopped down and walked through the scattered leaves to where he was working.

"What is that going to be?" Peggy asked.

Without looking around, Harry Randle unloaded a shovelful of dirt very close to her new shoes, but Peggy was ready for that and she didn't flinch. Instead she looked up at him in her peculiarly rapt and courteous way, willing as always to respond to any indication of goodwill.

Randle leaned his shovel against a wrought-iron signpost and wiped his perspiring forehead with the back of one hand. He smiled then, not really looking at her.

"It's for your dead cat," he said.

"I don't have a dead cat."

"I wouldn't be that sure."

"I'm sure; I don't. Do you mean Satch?"

Harry Randle didn't reply. He wasn't much older than some of the high school boys, as far as Peggy could tell, but he was a lot meaner. His remarks about her cat, even though she knew better than to believe him, worried her, so she looked here and there in the yard, hoping to find Satch in the best of health. Then she glanced toward the street, where Dr. Britton's station wagon was parked. She saw two wrapped evergreen shrubs in the back.

"*That's* what you're doing," Peggy said. "You're digging holes for the plants."

Randle lifted his shovel and jabbed it casually into the ground a few times, still smiling. "Dead cat makes good plant food, makes 'em *grow*."

"You're a faker. You wouldn't touch Satch."

"Better make sure he doesn't come around me again," Randle said seriously. "I almost got him last time." He lashed out with his shovel, smacking the flat blade against the ground. "Ha!"

Peggy edged closer to the hole, peered inside. Satisfied that it was empty, she started toward the house. Harry Randle was one of the doctor's regular hands on his farm, but he came over to the Connellys' once a week to do yard work and other chores Helen Connelly couldn't do herself. Peggy had long ago given up trying to be friends with Randle. Apparently he just didn't like little girls, something new in her experience.

Near the porch Peggy became aware that Randle was quietly following her and she turned quickly, frowning; but he wasn't up to anything.

"What are you jumping for?" he said, enjoying her discomfort. "As long as you're going inside, tell Dr. Britton I have to walk down to the Texaco station and pick up my car. I'll be back in a few minutes."

"OK," Peggy said, and she walked on unhurriedly to the glassed-in front porch of the two-story frame house. Her mother kept a few items on the porch—unwieldy spinning wheels and cider presses and occasionally a full-size wood-burning stove—but the porch wasn't cluttered. Unlike a lot of the antique dealers in The Shades, Helen Connelly had a real shop, not just a junk emporium. She also had steady clients from St. Louis and Kansas City, and places as far west as Oklahoma. Some decorators came as often as six times a year looking for rare buys, and although good antiques were becoming scarce in that part of the country, Helen had excellent contacts and was usually able to satisfy requests.

The foyer, living room and what had been a sun porch on the north side of the house were now filled with antiques. Peggy walked through the foyer—passing two display cases containing irresistible pieces of jewelry which she sometimes was allowed to touch, under supervision—dropped her school things on the stairway and entered the kitchen, which took up most of the rear of the first floor. Her mother was there, having coffee with Elsa and Andrew Britton.

3

"I hope it's going to turn *cold* tonight," Peggy said. "I'm tired of this hot weather." She began rummaging in the breadbox.

"I'm frying doughnuts here, 'less you're too impatient," said Brenda, the cook.

"I thought you had some fried already."

"A little cool weather and we won't be able to stir the tourists with a stick," Elsa Britton remarked sadly.

"We need a big fall tourist season," Dr. Britton said. "The rain this summer hurt more people than I can think of offhand."

Helen sugared her coffee and watched as Peggy stood on tiptoe to reach a carton of milk in the refrigerator. "Andy, have you heard any more about that plan to put a ski lift on Ben Lomond Mountain?"

"Ski lift!" old Elsa snorted. "What are they going to ski on? We don't have that much snow around here."

"Supposedly the people who build the ski lift will use a snow-making machine to keep the slopes covered."

"I know it's mostly St. Louis money," Andrew Britton said thoughtfully. "Same people who own that big resort on the Lake of the Ozarks. Hardly any hills at all up that way, and they've got a ski lift now."

"Well, they'll ruin the mountain," Elsa said, with a shake of her head. "Like that real estate outfit which got hold of Blue Eye Knob ruined *it*."

"I don't know," Helen murmured. "Most of the people who live up there are year-around, and that's fine for the town."

"The Shades was doing all right twenty years ago," Elsa replied, more pointedly than necessary.

4

"Before all the *year-arounders* moved in. Next thing, we'll have trailer parks and bowling alleys and teenage gangs running wild just like over at Table Rock two summers ago." She glared at her husband. "Somebody has to draw the line, or that's exactly what *will* happen. Ski lift! We've already got too many so-called artists around. Folk singers!"

"Them doughnuts is still hot, Peggy; don't cry to me when you burn your mouth."

"I don't think we're going to grow too fast," Dr. Britton objected. "Actually, with all we've got to offer here it's a wonder we haven't been overrun." He stretched and moved his chair around to be in the sun that came through the open back door. He was a short, muscular man of sixty-five who had lived in The Shades since the late nineteen twenties, a time when the valley and the surrounding mountains and ridges were almost inaccessible to all but the most dedicated sportsmen—and alcohol tax agents. "Long as people hold on to their property and don't let themselves get tempted by get-rich-quick promoters, we'll be all right. As for the artists, they're even more particular than the rest of us. They came here for the privacy and the natural beauty of the place, and they don't want to see it change either."

"Peggy, don't eat standing up," Helen said to her daughter.

"Dr. Britton, do you have any bees in your car?"

The doctor smiled. "Matter of fact, I picked up a shipment of bees, with queen, at the post office this afternoon—"

"How many?"

"I'd say there should be about fifteen thousand in the hive this time of the year."

Peggy sat down beside her mother and looked at him, enraptured. "What are you going to do with so many bees?"

"I'm going to train some of them."

Peggy was puzzled by the concept of trained bees. "Can I watch?"

"Sure, come over any time."

"Bees, Andy?" Helen said doubtfully.

"Perfectly safe," he assured her.

"What about that boy in Springfield who died from a bee sting this summer?"

"He was probably hypoallergic."

Peggy nodded thoughtfully. "Did you ever get stung?"

"Plenty of times."

"You'd better train the new bees not to bite, then," she advised him.

The telephone in the hall rang.

"That's Rosalind!" Peggy said.

"What'll I tell her?" Helen asked over one shoulder as she left the kitchen to answer the phone.

"Oh, tell her I'll be *delayed.*"

"Right," Helen said. She frowned at the school things piled on the stairs and picked up the receiver of the telephone, which was sitting on a meticulously refinished Sheraton table at the entrance to the living room.

"Auntie Helen?"

She was looking through the glass to the right of the door, looking beyond the porch at the yard, where Randle had left his shovel leaning against the sign that read "HELEN CONNELLY—ANTIQUES," and at first she wasn't certain just what she'd heard.

"Yes . . . hello? Is that you, Rosalind?"

"Auntie Helen . . ." She frowned; not a girl's voice. "Auntie Helen, I missed the school bus. Will you come get me?"

Wrong number, she thought. "Who is this?"

"It's Michael, Auntie Helen."

"What?"

"It's Michael."

Helen said nothing at all.

"Are you coming?"

"Just . . . a minute. Now, who *is* this?" But the connection was broken before she finished.

For several moments she continued to hold the receiver, her eyes fixed on the yard, on the street. A couple of kids went by on bicycles. Far away the ridges were a mass of yellow leaves, ripe for a stunning autumn show. The sky was blue and filled with lumbering clouds, and the sun blazed long shadows everywhere.

"OK," she said, half to herself, then replaced the receiver and went back to the kitchen.

"Did you tell Rosalind?"

"It wasn't Rosalind, sweetie." She sat down and stared at her half-empty coffee cup, then out the back door.

"You don't look too happy, Helen," Dr. Britton said.

"I just had a—" Her expression froze and she glanced quickly at her daughter, who apparently wasn't listening, but she went on in a more cautious tone of voice. "You know, one of those calls."

"Crank call?"

"Ah!" Elsa said, darkly, as if she were still thinking of artists and folk singers.

"No—I mean, that's not it exactly, Andy. I suppose it was just some sort of juvenile prank. It was a boy—about ten years old, I guess."

7

"What did he say to you?" Elsa demanded.

"He said—" Helen's mouth twisted in a bemused, half-sheepish way. "He said he wanted to be picked up. He was down at the school and he'd missed his bus, and he wanted me—"

"Is that all?" Elsa seemed disappointed. "You looked snakebit."

"In a way it was . . . cruel, because he, whoever that was, said he was Michael."

"Michael?" Dr. Britton repeated, and Brenda looked up from the stove.

"Michael."

Peggy finished her doughnut in the silence that followed, and glanced inquiringly at their faces. Dr. Britton smiled.

"Show you those bees now, honey?"

"I have to change my clothes," Peggy said, with a side glance at her mother, who nodded.

"Sugar on the mouth, Peg," she said absently.

Peggy swiped at her face with a napkin and took off, then remembered not to run and continued up the stairs two high steps at a time.

"Kind of an unlikely thing for a kid to do," Dr. Britton said when Peggy was out of hearing. "Calling up, pretending to be Michael. How many nine- or ten-year-old kids have heard of Michael Young?"

"I don't know," Helen said, and lighted a cigarette for herself.

"Well . . ." Elsa drawled, dismissing the matter. "Now that he's had his fun, no sense for you to be worried."

"I'm not worried." She smiled quickly, showing a dimple that in another woman of forty-five might have seemed frivolous. "But the strange thing—I just can't get it out of my mind—he called me

'Auntie Helen.' Nobody's ever called me that. Except Michael Young." She looked at them, perplexed. "Don't you think that's awfully strange?"

"Oh, now," Elsa said.

"I wonder why he did that?"

"Ask him when he calls again," Dr. Britton suggested, and fat Brenda, busy at her stove, cackled like a fiend.

2

Like ninety percent of the people who lived in
The Shades, Helen Connelly was not a native of
the area. Neither was she a "year-arounder,"
which was Elsa Britton's term for all recent settlers who were attracted by the carefully preserved wilderness and by the lively artists' colony.
Helen had been a Chicagoan and a debutante, and
at twenty she'd had a West Point chapel wedding.
Not quite a year later, her husband, who was the
number-three man in his class, died aboard a tor-
pedoed troop ship bound for North Africa.

She had spent the wartime years in Washington
and the years immediately following in New York,
working at a succession of "interesting" and
"challenging" jobs and it was a puzzle to her family and friends why she didn't remarry. To her
earnest suitors she gave the easy and the obvious
answer. One of them, however, saw her emotional

situation a little more clearly, and presumed to discuss it with her.

"You had it good with Ben and that was a damned lucky thing, because at that age it usually doesn't work for more than a few months, if at all—and believe me, I know, I was married myself then. It was, let's say, a perfect marriage, which is another way of saying a perfect mating; good sex keeps otherwise horrible marriages going longer than they have any right to. And fortunately—or was it so fortunate?—the marriage never suffered for any of the usual reasons, because it didn't last long enough. The day he died you loved him as much or more than when you married him. So now you're getting close to thirty and there's not another Ben in sight and never will be, and any marriage you might make is going to be subject to the usual stresses and discomforts: it will take a certain amount of work to make a new marriage livable no matter how good a guy you choose. And you can't face that. You can't face the prospect of years, and inevitable disappointments. You're in a fix, Helen, and I'm sorry for you."

And she had said simply, "I can't face not being in love the only way I know how to be," and that had sounded right to her. Months had passed before she began to doubt her reasoning, to attack her complacency and the carefully wrought illusions that had kept her alive and functioning for so long. In her mind she had preserved the precious, irreplaceable marriage in infinite detail, as if he might return at any moment. Was it wrong to cling to that beautiful year, was it cowardly? He will not come back, she told herself boldly. But she knew that, she knew it . . . and quite abruptly one winter afternoon she realized the truth, with a feeling of suffocation, of horror.

The phantom marriage she had preserved innocently, with devotion, was close to destroying her. It had become all the reality she needed to live on. There were moments when it seemed that if she concentrated long enough, then the year of her marriage would become a living thing, and all the years she had endured with bravery and dedication since Ben's death would fall from the galaxy of time; they would no longer exist.

She knew that this dislocation was the beginning of a severe nervous breakdown, perhaps a permanent breakdown, and she had no will to resist it. At least it would be a sweet form of insanity, a through-the-looking-glass escape from the inevitability of a wretched old age . . .

But her escape had been in a totally different direction; less than a week after discovering that she'd had only a tenuous contact with reality for much too long, she found herself, unwillingly, in The Shades, a place she'd never heard of, found herself involved in trouble that demanded all her time and strength. The months that followed had been harrowing, but through plain neglect the one-and-only marriage had dwindled to a proper distance in her thoughts, and after that, falling in love had been easy and natural. First she fell in love with The Shades itself, and then, much later, with Ed Connelly.

They were driving back from the post office in the village of The Shades when Peggy said, "Who's Michael, Mother?"

Helen was used to questions out of nowhere but she was sure she looked a little surprised at this one because Peggy said patiently, "The boy who called you a little while ago."

"Oh." Helen stopped at the state highway intersection, then continued on up White Church Road. "I don't really know who that was, Peggy; some little boy who should have better things to do than annoy people over the telephone."

"But you said it was Michael. Michael who?"

Helen hesitated, then explained with a smile, "Michael was your cousin Craig's brother, honey, but he died a long time ago. Before you were born. Cousin Craig was only eleven years old then."

"What happened to Michael?"

"He ran—ran away from home often, and the last time he ran away he got lost in a blizzard."

"Didn't anybody ever find him?"

"Yes, but it was weeks and weeks afterward." Helen pulled up in front of the house, parked her ranch wagon on the asphalt pavement which she'd provided for her customers and took the key out of the ignition. "So you see that wasn't Michael— my nephew Michael—on the telephone today. It was someone pretending to be." Helen was prepared for a thornier job of explaining but Peggy confounded her by dropping the subject.

"If Fletcher Ames finds a skunk and if he gives me the skunk, can I keep him?"

"No, I don't think so. Skunks aren't very good pets."

"Could I have a kitten?"

"I doubt if Satch would tolerate a rival around the place."

"Oh, Satch," Peggy said disparagingly. "He's not a *very good* pet. And he runs away *often*."

"That he does. Don't *you* run away. Brenda's go-

13

ing to have supper ready a little early this evening."

On weekdays during the fall season it was unusual for more than a dozen people to stop and browse and, as a rule, Helen closed her shop after two o'clock. But on this afternoon she had a late appointment with an old customer who collected milk glass, and while Helen was entertaining her, a car from Illinois pulled up and several elderly tourists asked if they could look around. They stayed until past dark and bought nothing, which was no surprise. Meanwhile Helen received two long-distance telephone calls, one from a decorator in Kansas City who *desperately* needed a blue-and-white oval hooked rug; the other call was from an undertaker's assistant in Steeleville who told her that an old and almost penniless spinster had died that afternoon in the community, leaving a houseful of gorgeous antique pieces which more than likely would be auctioned off as soon as the heirs could arrange it.

Helen hated this part of the business, but to stay in business at all she needed such informers. She questioned the mortician at length. He had been in the house, of course, and he was able to give her enough detail about the furniture to convince her that it was worthwhile making a bid for the lot. While the Illinois tourists wandered around complaining about high prices ("I can remember when them pitchers was so *common* you couldn't give 'em away!"), Helen did some hasty figuring in her small office just off the foyer. It was after banking hours in St. Louis, but she contacted a vice president of the Brentwood Bank with whom she was on friendly terms and found out how much she could borrow. Then she made one last call, to a lawyer in Salem, who would handle the transaction for her. The lawyer advised Helen that he knew the heirs, and he was morally certain that any of them Hustings would hunt wild pig with a hoe handle for the amount of money Helen was prepared to offer. So that was that. Helen made a note to send the mortician a money order for twenty dollars, washed her hands in the lavatory under the stairs and went happily to supper, which Brenda had been keeping hot for the past ten minutes.

Peggy was making a mound of her turnips to one side of her plate and discussing the ramifications of her latest falling out with Rosalind, who was Peggy's best friend when she wasn't being such a terrible baby, when the telephone rang again. Helen went to answer, noticing that it seemed colder in the house, as if the temperature outside was plunging.

"Hello?"

"Auntie Helen?"

Oh, God, she thought involuntarily, wincing, but she gained control of herself and said sharply, "I don't know why you think this is funny, but I'm not impressed and I want you to *stop calling here.* Do you understand?"

"Auntie Helen, why didn't you pick me up?" the voice said plaintively.

"Now, listen—"

"It's dark, and I can't walk home. My mother's going to be mad—"

"Who is this?"

There was no reply, but Helen heard a kind of sighing on the line that caused the skin of her forearms to tighten until she tentatively identified the sound as wind. She glanced outside and saw leaves flying through the nimbus of light from the lantern outside her gate.

"Please come," the boy said, and he sounded subdued, doleful. "What's wrong, Auntie Helen? Are you mad at me?"

"I'm not—" she started to say, but the connection was broken suddenly, as it had been earlier that day. Helen rubbed her forehead with her index finger, listening as if she half expected to hear the voice again despite the steady and familiar signal on the line; she put the receiver down unnecessarily hard.

"Now I'm getting mad," she said aloud, confirming it for herself, and Peggy called from the kitchen.

"Who was that, Mother?"

"A spook," Helen muttered, stopping to make an adjustment of the thermostat before she entered the kitchen. "Baby, are you warm enough in that sweater?"

"Yes," Peggy said. "What spook?"

Helen went to the stove to pour more coffee for herself. "That's just an expression. By spook I mean . . . a child who gets on people's nerves."

"Like Rosalind."

"Not like Rosalind. Rosalind's just— She doesn't mean to be a— Maybe we'd better skip it." Helen looked significantly at the pristine mound of turnips on Peggy's plate.

"I guess I wasn't in the mood for turnips," Peggy said with an analytical frown. "Like Michael?"

"What?"

"Was the spook you were talking to like Michael?"

"As a matter of fact it was. . . . The turnips tasted a little strong, didn't they?"

16

Peggy nodded. "It wasn't Brenda's fault, though."

"How about some blackberry cobbler?"

"Yes!"

"I'll dish up the cobbler while you carry your plate to the sink and wash it."

"Do you want me to carry your plate too?"

Helen looked at her unfinished dinner. "Might as well," she said glumly.

Peggy got up, cleaned her plate at the sink, then returned and put an arm commiseratingly around her mother's shoulders. "Whoever that is calling," she said with great severity, "I just wish he'd stop!"

"Oh, baby. It isn't anything, really. Don't you worry about it."

Helen was aware, however, that she had already communicated a good part of her irritation with the young prankster, and so she tried hard during the next two hours to divert Peggy and keep her mind off the telephone calls, off "Michael"—if indeed Peggy was thinking about him at all. Helen didn't know and considered it unwise to ask.

Twice before eight o'clock the telephone rang; each time she tightened up and struggled with feelings of dismay and anger before answering. But neither of the callers was "Michael."

Peggy went to bed a little later than usual, and for an hour afterward she was restless because of the pane-rattling, frost-bringing wind that roared through the narrows of the valley and poured leaves upon their roof. Once her daughter had settled down for good, Helen holed up in the office nook which she had outfitted with a rolltop desk and gradually, over the years, crammed with all

17

the treasures she had found it impossible to part with. There were three baroque lamps rewired for electricity, an assortment of candelabra, a wall of miniature paintings, bronze busts of children, ink-wells, glass paperweights, many photographs of glassy-eyed Victorians, a petit-point footrest and a framed autograph of Franklin Pierce. There were also stacks of fragrant, crumbling leather-bound books. All the objects seemed to share a comfortable, if down-at-the-heels immortality, and Helen found this atmosphere soothing whenever she found herself in difficulty with the monthly accounts.

About eleven the phone rang again, startling her. She had been absorbed in an expensive, beauti-fully photographed study of antebellum Louisiana mansions which a friend had loaned to her, and the wind had lulled her into a series of yawns. Helen sat up straight, and a dark bust of a child caught her eye.

"Time for all good little boys to be asleep," she said, looking again at the pendulum clock on the wall opposite her desk to check the time. And she felt a little worried, not because it might be the same boy calling again, but because she was automatically assuming, whenever the telephone rang, that it *was* him.

After all, he'd had his fun.

Yes, but, she thought, and hurried across the foyer to lift the receiver before Peggy woke up.

She heard someone crying.

You've had your fun, Helen tried to say, but she couldn't; her mouth had dried up.

He was weeping this time, heartbroken, and his sobs shocked her because it wasn't a child playacting; she was certain of that. He was terrified, helpless, alone.

"Auntie Helen—"

"Y-yes—"

"I'm . . . home . . . and there's . . . nobody . . . here."

"Oh, my God," Helen said quickly and harshly, "don't keep this up. Whoever you are, please—"

"There's . . . nobody here. Where's my mother?"

The wind outside, to which she had paid little attention for the last hour, suddenly turned on the house and thumped at the door. Helen fell back against the table, trembling.

'Where's *Craig*? Where's my brother?"

"Please," Helen whispered. "What are you trying to do?"

He was weeping again. She put the receiver down on the table and ran from it, into the kitchen. But the blackness outside the windows was too forbidding; she couldn't stay there. And it seemed she hadn't escaped him after all; she was still trembling, still vulnerable, and pathetically frightened for a mature woman who was sure that she knew a great deal about the foibles of children.

Yes, real children. But this one is a sadistic, depressing ogre.

When Helen felt she could breathe normally, she returned to the foyer and picked up the receiver of the telephone. She heard nothing this time except the sighing, the tricky fade and rise of the wind, somewhere.

I'm going to be rid of you, she thought. *I'm going to stop you if it takes*—"Hello," she said, and paused. "You wanted to talk to me. That's a good idea. I certainly want to talk to you." Again Helen paused. "I know you're still there, so why don't you say something? How long do you think—"

He screamed then, not in her ear but seemingly from a distance, and Helen cringed.

"Michael!" she said, not meaning to. "Mi—"

"I'm dead, aren't I? I'm dead, I'm *dead*!"

She hung up instantly, and seconds later tears formed in her eyes.

"Mother?" Peggy called from her room.

"Wha—what is it, Peg?"

"Who are you talking to?"

"I'm sorry if I woke you up. Please go back to sleep. It was only ... Reverend Bartlett. I was talking to him on the phone."

"You sounded loud."

"Yes. I'm sorry, baby. Good night."

"Good night."

Loud enough to wake Peggy, she thought, despairingly. Her heart still felt flogged and sore. This thing is really getting to me, and I'm going to have to— *It wasn't Michael*.

She looked up, startled by the denial that had so abruptly crossed her mind.

Of course it wasn't Michael, and I'm not haunted.

But I could use someone to talk to, Helen admitted bleakly, and reached for a brass box of cigarettes on the table beside the telephone.

While she was dialing she felt as if she might be surrendering something valuable of herself, surrendering self-reliance perhaps. She and Peggy had lived in their house, alone, since the death of Ed Connelly, and not once during those years had she given in to the need to call someone during a particularly lonely and difficult evening, to invite company. But this time—

Morning seemed a long way off, and she was too disturbed by the calls from "Michael" to wait that long to discuss them with a friend.

"Craig? I hate to bother you this time of night, but . . . You're not? Good. I'm afraid I have a— an odd sort of thing has happened here tonight and . . . Could you? Oh, I'd appreciate . . . No, don't come barreling down that road; it's not all that urgent."

Helen was surprised to feel considerably relieved after saying good-bye to her nephew. To hell with all that self-reliance, she thought cheerfully, and went into the kitchen to make coffee.

Craig Young was twenty-eight, which is not extremely youthful for a practicing psychologist, and many men have begun to mature strikingly near thirty, but to Craig's occasional chagrin he still looked very much like a college freshman. He was quite tall, over six feet four inches tall, and well-knit—in fact, he'd played excellent college basketball—but because he was mostly lengths and angles, he looked at a glance to be badly constructed, and therefore seemed ungraceful. Except for fuzz, most of the hair was gone from the front of his head, but a good many college boys these days are going bald. He had cultivated a moustache, which was sandy and incongruous. He smoked a pipe and was uncomfortable with it. Perhaps this mild self-consciousness had prompted him to accept a position at the nearby Greenleaf School, a semi-institution for difficult boys up to twelve years of age, instead of at a hospital or a university. Or perhaps, having grown up in The Shades, he loved the area too much to stay away for long.

"Whoever the boy is," Craig said, after pouring

his third cup of coffee, "it's obvious that he knows a lot about Michael, and about us."

"Too much."

"I suppose some of the people around here still talk about my mother, and Michael. Any impressionable kid has fantasies of running away and dying in a—well, in a romantic way far from home, so it's reasonable to assume your caller has let the whole story of the Youngs get the best of him."

"He's more than just an ordinary impressionable boy. He's fantastic, Craig."

"How do you mean?"

"He's convinced that he *is* Michael. Because what I heard over the telephone wasn't make-believe. He wasn't acting. Everything he said was pathetically real. And the way he sobbed!" Helen shook her head. "I wish I could remember the quality of Michael's voice . . ."

Craig tilted his chair back and smiled skeptically. "All ten-year-old boys tend to sound alike on the telephone. You're not hinting we have a ghost on our hands, are you?"

"He called me Auntie Helen," she replied, looking no less troubled than when Craig had walked in.

"So did I, while I was growing up."

"Oh, no," Helen said quickly. "You didn't. That was Michael. Only Michael. I'll have to admit our pretender has frightened me, but disregarding his ability and his motives for the moment, how could he possibly know to call me *Auntie* Helen?"

Craig thought about it, then spread his hands and grinned broadly. "All right, I'm stumped. But there *is* an explanation."

"Hmm," she said, unconsoled.

"I deal with troubled children; they've been my major interest in life for going on six years now. You're bewildered by this impostor who keeps calling you up and scaring the— And I don't blame you, but: bear in mind he is an impostor, and he'll get tired of his game, and take up something else. Sex, I hope."

"When will he get tired?"

"I don't know. I'm sorry to say, the more absorbed they are in their game, the more persistent they can be; speaking professionally, it sometimes takes months, or years, to separate a disturbed child from his fantasies and delusions."

Helen put her hands over her face, and groaned.

"Change your number, and don't give the new number to anyone but a few friends," Craig suggested.

"I happen to be in the antique business, and from time to time people *do* need to get in touch with me. Besides, it would be days before a new telephone could be installed." She lighted a fresh cigarette. "Who could it be? I think I know just about every boy and girl in The Shades, and I can't imagine any of them— Craig, do you suppose one of the boys at your school is making the calls?"

"Several of them have the depth of imagination and emotional instability necessary for such a fantasy to evolve, but none have access to a telephone, particularly at eleven o'clock at night."

"Don't they ever sneak out after dark?"

"Sure. Once or twice, until we get on to them and put a stop to it."

"He could have sneaked away from the school then, and—"

"Pinning it on one of our kids, eh?"

Helen sighed. "Just trying to come up with something halfway reasonable."

Craig stretched and got up to put his saucer and cup in the sink. "Want me to stick around tonight?"

"What? Oh, that's not necessary." Her eyes went to the stove clock and she stood up hurriedly. "I'm sorry, Craig. Twenty minutes to one—why didn't you shut me up half an hour ago?"

"Enjoyed it. Haven't been over for quite a while."

"How's Amy?"

"She's been away visiting her folks. I think she got back tonight."

"We're going to have an evening real soon," Helen promised, walking him to the front door.

Craig picked up his shearling coat on the way and put it on, yawning. "That wind's not going to quit till morning. Sometimes I think it'll blow me right off Ben Lomond. Tell Peg I'm sorry I didn't get to see her."

Helen went as far as the front porch with him, and waited outside, shivering, as he walked to the gate.

Inside, the telephone rang, but at first she didn't hear it because of the wind. When she did become aware of the telephone she started inside, changed her mind and yelled, "Craig!"

He looked up as he was about to get into his car.

"Telephone!" she said, pointing, and ran to answer.

Craig hesitated, then shut the car door and hurried back to the house. But Helen had let the door close behind her. He tried the knob and found that the door was locked. Then he considered ringing the bell, and quickly thought better of it. He peered in through the narrow glass to the left of the door. The foyer was dark but he could see her, standing at the edge of light from the kitchen, one hand on the table, the other holding the receiver of the telephone to her ear.

He rapped on the glass. "Helen!"

She turned and put down the receiver and came. When she opened the door her face was chalk, her eyes blank.

"That boy again?" he said, scowling.

"Yes, it was Michael."

"What? Now listen, Helen, you can't . . ." He took her arm and turned her from the doorway, entered the house himself. With the wind shut out, Craig could speak more quietly.

"Aunt Helen, that's not Michael, my brother Michael, who's calling you. Don't let yourself get in the habit of—" He stopped because she was paying no attention to him. "What did he say this time?" He gripped her arm more tightly and she responded with a wince.

"Oh, Craig, that hurts me!"

"I'm sorry," he apologized, letting go. "But you looked—"

"Don't worry, I'm really all right. This time he just—he said some things that—"

"What, Helen?"

"His voice was altogether different. So terribly cold. He— I think I want to sit down, if you don't mind." She went into the office and slumped in front of her desk while Craig filled the doorway.

"He couldn't have had much to say. You were only on the phone about half a minute."

Helen lifted her eyes. "All he said was, 'My

mother's dead, isn't she? Why did you send her away to die, Auntie Helen?' "

Craig was silent for half a minute, looking bleakly at her. He said finally, "This is one I'd like to write up, if we ever get hold of the lad who's making the calls. I suppose . . . I'd better notify the sheriff."

"What good will that do?"

"Well . . ." Craig shrugged, then admitted, "No good at all, I'm sure. I was hoping it might make you feel a little better."

"Good Lord, Craig, I'm not that upset!" After a moment she smiled, her face softening. "And I didn't mean to jump on you. I think I could use a good night's sleep."

"Before you go up, wrap the telephone in a thick towel and put it in the closet. If he's still in a talkative mood this late, let him wear his dialing finger out."

Helen nodded. "I know you can't predict how long this boy will keep calling, Craig. But do you think he'll . . . limit himself to calls?"

"What do you mean?"

"What if he gets the urge to—to come around?"

"I don't think that's likely, Helen."

"You can't be sure, can you?"

"Not without—"

"He was angry with me, Craig. He sounded betrayed." Helen stared at him, unable to keep the concern she felt from her face.

"Maybe . . . you and Peg should come up on the mountain with me for a few days if you don't feel safe here."

"That would mean a lot of explaining to Peg. So far she's not disturbed by the calls, and not more than normally curious. If Mi— If the boy keeps

26

calling, I should be able to ... Well, I think I'm prepared for almost anything; I'll just have to handle him the best way I can."

Craig said slowly, "I think there's a good chance you won't hear from him again. He more or less threatened you this last time, and accused you of doing away with his mother." Helen looked startled and dismayed, but Craig went on, eagerly. "That's good; it may have been the key to the fantasy which he constructed from elements of our lives. He's a boy whose mother died, or left him without explanation. Now he has an explanation, and he's fixed the blame. He doesn't need his fantasy anymore; no matter how long it took him to become 'Michael,' he can discard 'Michael' in an instant."

Helen studied him rather dubiously. "You're the psychologist. Not just trying to cheer me up, are you?"

Craig smiled guilelessly. "It's a reasonable theory. I'll go home and kick it around, unless you'd rather have me stay—"

"No, go home, for heaven's sake. In another thirty seconds I'll be yawning in your face."

"A dollar says you don't hear from him again."

"I'll believe you're the greatest psychologist in the world. I'll believe you can cast spells."

"Be around tomorrow night to collect my dollar," Craig warned her, heading for the door.

"Fine; and be prepared to stay for supper, or Peg will lose faith in all cousins."

He bent to kiss her forehead, then walked into the wind, chin down. Helen ducked back inside, letting go the yawn she had threatened him with. She stayed downstairs just long enough to put out the lights, thinking about Craig's moustache and wondering how long it would be before Amy got him to shave it off; thinking about the dollar bet. All that Craig had surmised about the telephoning boy sounded logical. She was content to believe he was right, as she started up the stairs.

And the telephone rang.

Damn you!

Her jaw set, Helen snatched up the receiver.

"Hey, Bertram! Hey, old buddy!"

"Friend," Helen said, "thank you for having the wrong number.'

3

The Greenleaf School was located a couple of miles from the village center in an area which old settlers still referred to as Eveningshade: a hollow about half a mile long hemmed in by sometimes vertical ridges four hundred to a thousand feet high. The floor of the hollow had been cleared and planted in grass for athletic fields and the school buildings formed a rough quadrangle atop the southernmost ridge overlooking the fields. They were expensive fieldstone buildings, approximately twenty years old. There was a wall around the quadrangle, a low wall which served to enhance the campus rather than to keep people at a distance, or to restrict the students, most of whom came from well-to-do families. As a rule it took a great deal of money to send a boy to the Greenleaf School for a year, but most of the parents who had sons at Greenleaf were sufficiently desperate not to care what it cost. In addition to topflight teachers experienced in dealing with bright but undisciplined children, there were also two psychiatrists and two clinical psychologists on the staff. Both psychiatrists commuted once a week from St. Louis, which was 140 miles away. Consequently Craig Young and his assistant, Amy Lawlor, did most of the work with the two dozen boys who required regular therapy.

They were having a late lunch in the faculty dining room when Craig mentioned the telephone calls his aunt had received the day before. Amy was immediately intrigued and pressed him for details.

"One of our gentlemen?" she suggested, when Craig had told her all he knew.

He packed his pipe with tobacco and lighted it, talking between puffs. "Helen thought so, but I couldn't go along with her. We've got missing-parent syndromes, all right. But I can't believe any of our boys have ever heard of my brother Michael. After all, that was sixteen years ago. Who still talks about him? *I* don't; I hardly think about Michael. I doubt if any of the locals remember him well; the story's not all that interesting."

"The boy who called Helen certainly knew a lot about Michael, and his fantasy was beautifully organized. Morbid too. If I were Helen I'd have climbed the walls."

Craig said cheerfully, "He hasn't called today, though; I was talking to Helen just before I came down to eat. So the hunch I had last night might be accurate: the boy doesn't need 'Michael' anymore, and he's dropped him."

Amy poured half a glass of iced tea for herself. She was a year younger than Craig, a tall blond girl with a good figure and a quiet-seeming face made extraordinary by the kind of wicked downy eyes so many Hollywood starlets have. She'd been a starlet herself, briefly, before discovering that she didn't have quite enough talent to justify the grueling process of becoming an actress.

"That's probably the answer," Amy said after thinking it over, "but your aunt was convinced that Michael was real."

"She didn't know what to think."

"Craig . . . you don't believe in spirits, but—"

"Damn right I don't."

"But," Amy said firmly, "I do."

Craig groaned, then smiled at her. "Nothing supernatural about this at all."

"Oh, no? I think we could build a strong case for the supernatural."

"Go ahead, build a case. Are you going to finish your pie?"

"Help yourself. Craig, you've assumed that the caller is a boy who has so familiarized himself with the story of your brother that he has actually come to believe he is Michael. But on the other hand you admit it's improbable that a boy who is, say, ten years of age could learn that much about another boy, dead for sixteen years."

"Improbable; not impossible."

"I'll concede that point. But this boy called Helen 'Auntie Helen,' and she swears no one but Michael Young ever called her that."

"Probably not less than a hundred people heard Mike say 'Auntie Helen' when he was alive."

"I won't concede there. It's not the sort of . . . verbal idiosyncrasy that's likely to be remembered."

Craig forked in the last of the cherry pie and

looked at her indulgently. "What's your solution?"

"It could be that the spirit of your brother Michael—"

"Picked up the telephone and called Helen a few times. What telephone? Where? In that astral waiting room the occultists are always talking about?"

"If you just want to have a good laugh—"

"No, no, I'm sorry. I'm listening. Please tell me."

Amy sighed and decided she wasn't very angry, and smiled slightly, but she was completely serious as she continued. "The spirit of your brother might be possessing another, outwardly normal boy here in The Shades. A boy with latent psychic-sensitive qualities."

"Demonic possession? If there *was* such a boy, it wouldn't be any secret. His parents would have brought him to us in a bag to have his demon exorcised, or whatever you do with demons."

"No. The boy I'm thinking of might be puzzling his parents by acting . . . differently; but it wouldn't be cause for alarm unless Michael, the spirit Michael, greatly upset his host, or made him do wild things. That's not what Michael wants, however. He just wants to be in touch with his aunt."

"Good Lord, Amy, where'd you pick up all that witchcraft?"

"A friend of mine at UCLA was a spiritualist-medium. He was also a cracking good psychiatrist. He doesn't doubt that some forms of mental illness are caused by demons, and neither do I."

"Run across any demons lately?"

Amy gestured lightly toward the campus. "About one hundred thirty of them."

"Otherwise."

"I've never met any demons, I'm happy to say, and I've never seen a ghost. But I've *heard* plenty of spirits speaking their minds at séances." Craig had his scoffing look again, and Amy smoothed hair over one ear with the palm of her hand. "Now you have another theory of the telephone calls, and I believe my theory might be worth following up."

"Do you feel like a drive?"

"Sure. You mean you *are* taking me seriously?"

"I'm greatly interested."

"That's something," Amy murmured.

"In getting away for an hour with my girl," Craig said, grinning.

Once they were in his Chevelle and on the road to town—a narrow rumpled band of blacktop through heavy woods which Craig called "blind alley"—he had a couple more questions about Amy's preoccupation.

"If it is Michael's ghost, where has he been for sixteen years?"

"Can't tell you, because I don't know that much about the spirit world."

"Could he have been right here, in The Shades?"

"You'd like for me to say that's farfetched, but there are well-documented cases of spirits remaining quite near the place where the physical body died."

"So he could be around, but, being a spirit, he's invisible."

"Not necessarily. If he came into the presence of a psychic-sensitive, that person would know immediately. He might even be able to see the spirit as plainly as I see you now."

"Do you know any medium?"

"Not locally. Why?"

"Just curiosity. I've never been to a séance."

She grinned. "An honest medium might make a believer of you in a hurry."

"Don't bet on it. Where are we going; do you have your druthers?"

"Why don't we drive up Big Enoch to the Military Park?"

After the freeze of the night before the afternoon had a pleasant warmth and the sky was clear, almost iridescent blue. Craig drove with the top down and after they passed through the village he doubled his speed. Amy's long hair whipped like a pennant behind her and she smiled delightedly as they blazed through shadowy hollows red with sumac and darted around steep cliffs flawed by huge limestone outcroppings. They passed a timber dam and an old iron bridge below which the clear water ran four feet deep and clean enough to drink. Craig was saying something to her but Amy couldn't hear, and she waved for him to slow down.

"We used to live near here," he shouted. "Up that ridge. House is still mostly standing. Want to have a look?"

Craig never had had much to say concerning his boyhood; the talk at lunch about Michael and Michael's fate had greatly increased Amy's curiosity about the unhappy and tragic Young family. She was pleased but a little surprised that Craig was opening up this way, volunteering at last to share what had been a very private part of his life.

Amy nodded, and he slowed almost to a stop before turning at a point where a runneled gravel road came down to meet the county hard road.

There were three mailboxes beside the blacktop and as they went by Amy glanced at them. The last of the mailboxes was virtually rusted out but there was a hint of a name still visible on the uphill, weather-protected side of the box. YOUNG.

The road was quite steep and Craig had to use care in getting the car through the ruts and over the sizable rocks jutting out of the hard earth. On the left side of the road the woods had been selectively logged nearly to the top of the ridge and the remaining trees were big and widely spaced, with sun on the cleared ground between them. To the right the woods were almost impenetrable; they seemed cold despite the orange and scarlet tones of the leaves.

"Don't know who lives there," Craig said, pointing out an unpainted board house as they went by. "Summer people, I suppose. And the Crofutts live down at the end of that road, or they did the last time I was up this way."

"When was that?"

"I don't know," he replied, looking inexplicably glum. "Months, or years."

He drove another five hundred feet over the steadily worsening road and then turned cautiously and proceeded through underbrush almost as dense as a hedge which choked off the last ruts; they reached a stony clearing at the very top of the ridge. Looking back, Amy could just make out the highway below, and in front of her, through the mile-long break in a succession of razorback ridges known as Clark's Gap, she was able to see nearly all of the valley of The Shades—ten, perhaps twenty square miles, blocks of yellowed pasture alternating with fiery autumn woodland.

"Beautiful," she murmured. "What a wonderful place to live."

"I always thought so." Craig got out of the car, slipped his sunglasses into his shirt pocket and walked toward the abandoned cottage. Halfway there he turned his head quizzically. "You coming? Not much to look at, actually."

She joined him and they stood in front of the east-facing cottage. The roof was half gone, and so was part of one wall; blackened stones were scattered over a large area. Dried moss was thick everywhere, even on the exposed timbers. There were black shards of glass in a few windows. A tall oak which had partly burned along with the cottage still hung protectively, but in a crippled way, over the remains.

Amy stared at the cottage until a squirrel scampered fatly along the roof line. Then she looked up at Craig, who had not taken his eyes from her face.

"As you can see, it burned," he said.

"What happened?"

"Mother. She wasn't the most competent person under ordinary circumstances, but when she drank she was a disaster. We only had the fireplace for heat up here—enough on even the worst winter nights, you understand. But fires need tending, and Mother had the habit of heaping too much wood on the embers and then falling asleep on the sofa. The night the house burned some sparks popped out on the floor. It was lucky she woke up at all, but she did, and got us out through the back door. There's nothing to show you inside; it's just a shell. Melting snow from the roof put the fire out, or I'm sure there wouldn't be a trace of the house today."

Amy looked toward the other side of the clearing and saw a certain amount of litter: paper and tin cans. "Looks like a popular picnic spot. Who owns the property now, Craig?"

"I do. I inherited it at twenty-one."

Amy walked closer to the house. "This is where Michael said he was when he called your aunt late last night. I wonder—"

"For God's sake, Amy," he said dourly. "Let's go. I don't want to hear any more about ghosts."

Amy caught up with him before he reached the car. "I was being thoughtless," she apologized. "I know you didn't have a very happy time in this place."

He looked steadily at her, his eyes expressionless. "You're wrong, Amy. Michael and I were happy. Very happy, I'd say." He leaned back against the Chevelle and took out his pipe, gazing at The Shades through Clark's Gap. "We more or less ran wild in the woods, and we got along fine with Mother—treated her like an older sister. I know a lot more about her today than I did then, of course, and I can see her faults. She drank, and she . . . had no judgment when it came to men, and she neglected us half the time, but we didn't consider her absences neglect. We always knew if she wasn't here one day she'd be here the next, cooking, washing our clothes, trying to get us to wash, taking a fond interest in whatever we happened to be interested in. Seems to me even now that she was very happy, too, although I know better."

"She sounds as if she was a lovely person in spite of her weaknesses."

"We both know incipient manic-depressives can be terribly charming until they hit their low periods. Michael and I didn't see many of those;

37

Mother had the wisdom to keep away. Maybe she realized she might be the death of us during one of her spells. I suppose the only other wise decision she made was to get in touch with Aunt Helen when all the wrong turns in her life began leading straight to psychosis."

Amy moved closer to him, and rested her head against his shoulder.

"What happened to your mother, Craig?"

"After the house burned, Helen decided that Mother was a danger to herself and to us, so—well, she tried to persuade my mother voluntarily to enter Kempton Sanitarium for treatment. But Mother was deathly afraid of places like that. It was necessary to commit her. She died just a few hours after being admitted to Kempton, died of a collapsed blood vessel in her brain while struggling to escape. She was twenty-nine years old."

"That's dreadful."

"She was one of the doomed people we run into from time to time in our work. You feel in your bones as soon as you set eyes on them that they're going to die very young. I suppose Michael had that look, although I can't remember so very much about him. He was Mother all over again: dark, intense, filled with energy, wild and moody." Craig chuckled unexpectedly. "I don't know who I look like, unless there was an uncle Pastiche on the family tree somewhere."

"*I* like the way you look," Amy said, nestling, eyes closed. "Don't go knocking my guy."

Craig put his arm around her. "Meet any interesting men in California?"

"Dozens."

"Are they in love with you?"

"They were when I left."

"Shouldn't have left," he said, shaking his head.

Amy backed off, looked darkly at him and said, "Sometimes I'm not so sure when you're joking and when you're not."

"Oh, I'm joking."

"Do you wish I hadn't come back?"

"Don't be silly, Amy."

"I've been waiting all day for a welcome-home kiss, and I still haven't gotten one."

He made a move toward her, sheepishly; she walked back two more steps and said, her eyes still dark and a little hurt, "Too late when I have to ask."

Craig didn't seem to know what to do or say.

"Craig, are we going to get married?"

"I hope so."

"That's something. When?"

"When do you want to get married?"

"When do *you* want to?"

"Tonight," he said.

"No, you don't."

"What are we doing?" Craig said, blinking at her, amiable and perplexed. "We'll both get winded running around in circles like this."

"We've known each other a year and a half," Amy said deliberately. "And I've known that I love you for almost a year now. Six months ago I was sure you were in love with me. Today I'm not sure at all, and I wonder what happened. Don't I wear well? Am I using the wrong bleach? Have I lost my figure?"

Craig smiled meaninglessly.

"Well, *what*?"

"Amy, I love you very much."

"Either you're lying to me, or else you're taking me for granted."

"I don't think so."

"Maybe," she said angrily, "I've been making too many overnight trips up Ben Lomond Mountain. Is that the trouble, Craig?"

"You know damned well . . . there's no trouble, Amy. I want you as much as I ever have."

She hung her head. "You say it. But I don't feel it."

"I guess . . . we should be getting more definite about marriage."

"Too late when I have to remind you!"

He grinned. "Oh, no, it's not."

Amy poised to run. "Don't think you're going to grab me and—"

Craig lunged at her, and she ran for the nearest tree. He let her think she was going to reach it, then caught up in two strides and pinned her, struggling, against the trunk. Amy kneed his thigh with a ferocious expression but managed not to hurt him. Craig held her easily with one hand and stroked her with the other.

"You've got beautiful eyes," he said gravely. "Should be in pictures."

"I was."

"Prove it."

"Second lead in *Hollywood Blood Beasts*!"

"Believe I saw that one," Craig said. "About fifty times." He kissed her cold cheeks and then, with all the feeling she claimed to have missed, kissed her mouth. Amy was pleased to drop the pretense of a struggle.

After a while they went arm in arm back to the car, both of them flushed. Her hair had bark in it.

"Ben Lomond, here we come," Amy said dreamily.

"Well . . . later, I'm afraid. I'm going to be tied up at the school until around nine."

"Later it is," she vowed.

Amy had her hair combed out by the time they reached the bottom of the ridge, and they were both in high spirits during the drive back. Amy had forgotten completely about Michael Young, the telephone calls and the ruined cottage when Craig said abruptly:

"He must have been on the ridge having a picnic with his family, and heard the story from them."

"Who?"

"The boy who was calling Helen. That's the obvious place for him to have become intrigued by the saga of the Youngs. Well, it's over now. He's through calling." Craig's jaw was set. "He'd better be."

"For Helen's sake I certainly hope so. She didn't have an easy time trying to raise you two, did she?"

"I don't think I gave her much trouble. But Michael wouldn't have anything to do with Helen. I guess he thought she was responsible for our mother's death, and I couldn't make him change his mind. He kept running away, and I'd go after him, and somehow I always found him before he got too far. He put up some terrific fights, but even though I was only about a year and a half older I was a lot bigger, so I'd bring him back. Then one night, I'd say about ten months after Mother died, he ran off right into the teeth of one of the worst blizzards ever to hit down here, and that night I never had a chance. He wasn't found until early spring, deep in a hollow about five miles from here. He was just bones in a creek bed. And that was that. I went away to school the next fall; only made it back to The Shades during the summers and at Christmas. Probably just as well. I might have brooded about Mike otherwise."

"You did everything possible to help him."

"Did I?" He smiled, or grimaced. "Well, I wasn't very old either, and I didn't know how to handle Michael when he was in a fit of despondency. We were close, for brothers, but he just shut me out those times; shut me out."

"You have that tendency yourself, you know."

"What?"

"To shut people out. And when that happens to me, *I* don't know how to handle it. I get panicky."

"I'm sorry, Amy. Tonight will be different."

"Yes," she said. "I'm counting on that."

The brown-and-white pup came bounding up out of a ditch beside the road and Helen had to twist the steering wheel sharply to avoid running over him. Her ranch wagon veered to the far side of the road before she could bring it under control again. Elsa Britton pushed herself off the dashboard with a gasp.

"Oh, Elsa, I'm so sorry. Are you hurt?"

"Nah, nah, no damage." She shot a look at her friend. "Your face is whiter than that sweater. Wasn't such a close one."

"I hate to admit it, but I've got a case of nerves."

"Didn't sleep so good last night?"

"Didn't sleep, period."

"At our age, we can't afford sleepless nights and keep our looks," Elsa said stoutly, and Helen smiled; Elsa was sixty-three.

Elsa reached over and patted her shoulder. "Don't you worry; Craig knows about cranks and mental cases. You won't hear from that boy again."

"So far I haven't, but I wish I could be sure he won't call."

"It worries you, bring Peg and come on over to the place tonight."

"What worries me . . ." Helen murmured, coming to a stop in front of her house.

"How's that?"

"Elsa, first thing Peg wanted to know this morning was, did Michael call?"

"Naturally."

They got out, and Helen went around to unlock the tailgate so she could lift out the matching pair of Hepple-white side chairs she had bought earlier in Gladden.

"And she wanted to see a photograph of Michael."

"Do you have one?" Elsa asked, helping her with the chairs.

"I wasn't sure when she asked, but I thought if I could show Peg a snapshot of him it might get her off the subject, so I rummaged in a couple of old albums and found a school photo of Michael, taken when he was in the fourth grade." Helen leaned on one of the chairs and looked off down the street. The sky was still blue but it was beginning to get dark.

"Was she satisfied?"

"Elsa, Peg took one look at the photograph and said 'Oh, yes, I've seen him.' "

"Naturally," Elsa said. "She has a perfectly good imagination."

"I don't believe it was a story. Peggy sounded very sure, and she took the trouble to explain that it wasn't one of the boys at school she had in mind. This boy—Michael—doesn't go to The Shades School."

"Where did she see him?"

"On the school playground. Remember last week when she stayed after classes for reunion rehearsals, and I was an hour late getting back from Jack Creek? She was by herself on the playground until dark: I mean, she was alone except for the boy. He came within a few feet of her, Peggy said, but when she turned and saw him he ran for the woods."

Elsa smiled serenely. "She has a good imagination."

"I suppose he could have come from Greenleaf," Helen mused, "but at that time of day surely they have all of their boys accounted for. Elsa, how well do you remember Michael?"

"I remember him very well." She picked up one of the battered chairs. "I also remember his funeral," she said emphatically.

"I can get those in the house without any trouble," Helen protested. "Andy'll be wondering what's happened to you. Thanks so much for going with me today, Elsa."

"Ah, I enjoyed it," Elsa said. "Please do me one favor and stop thinking about ghosts."

"I haven't been. But I've been thinking an awful lot about coincidences. Now go on, Andy'll be calling here and giving me what-for."

"Won't even know I've been gone," Elsa said. "He'll be painting the equipment shed or fooling with his bees, and I'll have to shoot off a gun next to his ear to let him know dinner's ready. Never saw a man daydream like Andy. Good night, Helen. Call me up tonight if you have the chance."

Helen watched until Elsa had driven away in her vintage Plymouth, and then she picked up one of the chairs and lugged it as far as the porch, where she met an anxious Brenda.

"Supper's ready to go, and I called and called that Peg, but she ain't even answered."

"Do you know where she is, Brenda?"

"Sure! Perched in her tree house. Won't answer me though."

"Well, I'll get her in. Go ahead and serve, Brenda."

Helen left the first chair on the porch, hurried back for the other, locked her car and went around the house to the backyard. It was now getting dark enough so that she had to watch her step to keep from twisting an ankle on a hickory nut.

"Peg!" she called as she approached the tree house, and when her daughter didn't answer, wondered if Brenda had been right about her whereabouts.

Then she heard Peggy sob.

4

The Britton's farm, one of the best in The Shades, lay on the eastern slope of Blue Eye Knob, some four miles from the village. At one time Andrew Britton had been the only doctor in The Shades. Then the nearest hospital was a difficult forty-three miles away. Now the community had a thirty-bed hospital and three young physicians, in addition to Andrew, who saw patients only one day a week in the clinic which he had founded. Two days he devoted to his farm, but a good manager looked after the dairy herd and kept them solidly in the black.

This left Dr. Britton considerable free time to devote to hunting and fishing and to another hobby, apiculture.

One of the four substantial barns on the property had been converted into a huge apiary, the environment of which was as rigidly controlled as that of the dairy barns. For part of the afternoon the doctor had been unloading bales of hay with the help of Harry Randle, the only one of the hired hands who had no fears about stepping inside the barn, which at times contained upward of a half million bees.

In several ways Randle was a puzzle to the doctor. He had been working there almost a year; except for the farm manager, Sam Claypool, Harry was the best man Dr. Britton had. He was never late and never "sick," and he worked hard for his wage. He could repair several kinds of machinery and he knew how to handle the most intractable cows, which is an art not easily come by. What Harry didn't know about dairy farming he picked up effortlessly, and Dr. Britton had decided that Harry might make a good assistant for Claypool. At the same time he was hesitant to offer the promotion, because of things he'd heard about Harry Randle, and other things he'd observed for himself.

"Six of my hives are already on a winterized basis," the doctor explained as the two men were putting the hay bales in the barn. "Most of the workers are dead, and the drones were dragged out of the hives weeks ago, to die."

"Seem to be quite a few flying around," Randle said, hesitating a step as a bee skimmed past his nose.

"Those are scout bees, from the hives that are feeding regularly and will keep on feeding through the winter. But they won't bother you, and there aren't very many of them."

They stacked the bales and paused for a few moments to catch their breath.

"Air's full of them," Randle observed, but he

didn't appear to be bothered. "How do you know they're not getting set to swarm all over us?"

Dr. Britton chuckled. "They wouldn't unless we interfered with them—cut them off from their food supply, for instance. But a bee has a little clock inside of him that tells him when it's time to eat. That won't be for hours yet, until I put out their food dishes. Before then you'd have to set the hives on fire to get the workers into the air. Have you ever been around beehives, Harry?"

"A few summers ago."

"Where was that? I don't believe you've ever said where you're from."

"No, I never have," Randle replied, not looking at the doctor. Britton regarded him steadily, in a friendly way. Harry took off his khaki baseball-style cap and scratched at his dark close-cropped hair. Presently he smiled, yielding slightly to the doctor's interest in him. "I've lived a good many places. One suited me about as well as another."

"You had to be born somewhere."

"Yehp. I was born somewhere." He turned his deep-set eyes on the doctor, still smiling; it was no more than a mannerism at times, effective as a mask. "But I don't know where. I was born, and I got left, and I got raised up. Like everybody else. And when I got tired of one place, I moved."

"You must like it here in The Shades. Because you've stayed almost a year now, isn't it?"

"Yehp," Harry said, smothering a yawn to indicate his dislike of the doctor's probing. "It's all right here. Maybe we'd better fetch the rest of those bales before dark."

The two men walked slowly out of the barn.

"I don't mind telling you," the doctor said, "that I'm more than happy with the work you've done for us. Sam and I have had some talks. Sam could use an assistant. He'd like to have you, if you're willing."

"Oh," Harry said, grinning, but that was all he said until they had carried another bale apiece into the barn. Then he wiped dust from one cheek and looked speculatively at the doctor.

"I wouldn't be interested."

"Mind telling me why you wouldn't be?"

"I might decide to move on in a month or so," Harry answered vaguely. "Can't tell right now."

"I see. I thought it might be the idea of accepting responsibility for once."

Randle shrugged.

"Well, you're—what—twenty-six years old, Harry. You can't go on wandering for the rest of your life. This isn't the biggest dairy farm around, but it offers an opportunity. And I know you're not a lazy man. I'd like to see you tackle something a little more demanding than you've done up to now."

Harry dropped the smile and looked moody. "Why?"

"Because it would be good for you. Because you've got the native intelligence to be a good farm manager. And the ability to build a farm of your own someday."

Randle laughed shortly. "No, thanks!"

Dr. Britton smiled sadly at him. "Are you sure, Harry?"

"I like to work awhile, then do nothing awhile. I don't like being pinned down. No, thanks."

"OK." They went out again, into the fading sunlight. And the doctor said, "As long as we've come to grips, so to speak, I'd like to offer a little advice, Harry."

49

"Sure," Harry said, but not as if he liked advice; he looked a little stiff-necked.

"You have a prison sentence not too far behind you, isn't that right?"

Harry Randle hesitated, briefly, as he was about to haul another bale out of the pickup truck. "I expect you know as much about that as there is to know," he said easily. "Yehp. Three years. I stole a car." He seemed, if anything, a little proud of this.

"And you were in all kinds of trouble before that, as a juvenile. Well, the point I'm trying to make is, trouble's a difficult habit to break. Maybe you don't actively look for trouble, but you seem to favor the kind of drinking places where trouble is always available. Like the Thunderbolt Café. They had a knifing in the Thunderbolt Friday night, I hear. Oh, I realize you weren't involved. But—"

"Look," Harry said tensely, his expression harsh for a few moments. He looked as if he were about to drop the bale he was carrying and simply walk away, for good. But his protective smile edged back into place and he took a fresh purchase on the bale, saying, without anger, "I only work for you eight—ten hours a day. Rest of the time is mine. I know how to stay out of trouble. I know how to mind my own business. And I don't want any permanent jobs. I'll look out for myself, Doctor, if that's OK."

Dr. Britton wasn't offended, but he didn't want to antagonize Harry either, so he let the matter drop. He had no intention of letting Harry drift away without making every effort to help him. "Like you say. Let's get done here, Harry."

For his age the doctor was a strong and finely

conditioned man and he enjoyed the work, but it was past dark by the time they had completely unloaded the truck and placed the bales against the steel sides of the barn, where they would serve as insulation through the winter.

"Leave the truck by Sam's house when you go down the hill. Getting real foggy out, isn't it?" Ground mist was quite common four out of five autumn nights in The Shades: the roof of his house fifty yards away seemed to be floating on the heavy motionless mist, with the lighted windows looking like pale indistinct flares.

Once Harry Randle was gone Britton went back inside the barn, shutting the steel door after him. The lights overhead were powerful and placed to eliminate shadows. They remained on twenty-four hours a day. He walked slowly across the tanbark-covered floor to a series of tables which contained positioning hives painted blue, yellow, black and white, the colors bees found most easy to distinguish. On other tables there were feeding stations, painted and unpainted.

A few scout bees were hovering around the empty dishes; as Britton smiled, one of them took off and flew across the barn to the occupied hives a hundred feet away. When he turned back to the tables he felt something unusual and unpleasant: a gust of cold air.

There was a second door in the back wall of the barn and from where he stood the doctor could see that it was standing open a few inches. He scowled; that door was almost always locked, from the inside, and he used it seldom. He walked quickly to the door, opened it wide and looked out.

Behind the barn was a slope of about thirty feet,

a few young trees and the new road that twisted up Blue Eye.

The road was invisible in the mist, and the trees were vague presences.

Most of the regular hands on the farm, not liking bees, stayed out of the barn unless they had excellent reasons for being there. Britton wondered who had come in during the day and found it necessary to unlock the back door ... or perhaps the door had been unlocked for days, and he had never thought to check it. At any rate there seemed to be no point in tracking down the negligent hand, although if the door had blown wide open on a cold night it might have meant trouble for some of his bees. He was mildly angry as he set the lock.

Nearby was a florist's refrigerated display case, empty now, and a curious-looking prefab building approximately twelve feet by ten feet, with three ordinary sash windows set into the front of it. From here the doctor watched his swarming bees, sometimes with a high-powered pair of German binoculars. The building also contained a worktable, shelves, a filing cabinet and a beehive, the most recent addition to his apiary.

The wall-mounted telephone in his workroom was ringing as he opened the wooden door at one end. Dr. Britton picked up the receiver.

"Andy? I Just got home, so I'm afraid supper won't be until six-thirty at the earliest."

"That's all right; give me time to mark some bees. How was Helen?"

"Still acting snakebit."

"That's too bad. More calls?"

"No. I expect that's over with, and she'll be all right in a couple of days."

"I hope so. Well, ring me when you're ready."

After talking to Elsa the doctor settled down to work. From an open shelf containing many similar bottles and jars he selected an amber bottle with a spray attachment, labeled chloroform. Then he opened several small cans of paint and laid out his delicately tipped brushes on the worktable. "Marking" or numbering bees so that individuals could be traced in a swarm was a fairly simple if tedious job. First the entire colony was put to sleep so the necessary bees could be selected. Then, using an elementary color code—red for 1, yellow for 2, and so on—the doctor could number up to six hundred bees with just five colors, dabbing the shellac-base paint on the thorax or abdomen of each bee. The paint would stay bright and wear for weeks, and from the windows of his prefab building he could observe their flights to and from the hive as he changed the locations of feeding dishes and secondary hives from day to day.

The beehive on his table was nothing more than a square wood box with frames that slipped in and out, and a removable top. The bees had built their combs within the individual frameworks and, during spring and early summer, the relatively small hive might hold as many as seventy thousand bees. But now it was fall and as he had told Peggy Connelly, Dr. Britton expected to find no more than fifteen thousand bees grown to maturity after the height of the summer foraging season.

He tied a white gauze surgeon's mask over his mouth and nose, slid back the lid of the hive, picked up a magnifying glass in one hand and the bottle of chloroform in the other and began carefully to spray the inside of the hive.

He did not see the first bee that escaped and stung him, but he wasn't unduly disturbed—sometimes an individual bee wasn't immediately affected by the anesthetic and flew blindly to the light, and it was a mild sting, scarcely more than a pinprick. Despite the mask, he had been holding his breath, so he stepped back for a few moments to give the chloroform a chance to penetrate the cells of the comb. Then he reached out to slide the lid open a little more.

A great gout of black bees seemed to leap from the interior of the hive to fasten on his uncovered hand and wrist, and a numbing shock hit him immediately. He jerked his hand back and the hive toppled from the table, cracking open, the lid falling off.

In agony he brushed at the clot of bees on his hand, scattering a score of them. But already hundreds more were rising from the damaged hive. He stared in disbelief, first at the bees, then at the bottle of chloroform in his hand. He pulled the mast from his face and smelled, not chloroform, but the odor—the stench—of ripe bananas.

With a cry of terror the doctor turned and started for the door, but the unexpected banana scent clung to him, and the bees were all around him, as they would swarm around any intruder threatening their hive.

By the time he reached for the door he could no longer feel the individual stings on his neck and head: it was as if he had been seared by a blowtorch.

Then they were at his eyes.

Dr. Britton was screaming as he smashed into

the door and fell to the tanbark outside. He was a beeman and he knew he was going to die, but horror and a mighty instinct for survival kept him going. He rolled and fought the bees, but there were too many of them. Each time he struggled to his feet they drove him down again. He had aroused them and they were furious. They had blinded him, and deafened him. They were wedged in his nostrils and in his open mouth. They covered him like a hideous mask, like a living shirt.

He fell again, and was still.

Elsa was about to put the steaks under the broiler when the telephone in her kitchen rang.

She wiped her hands on her apron and picked up the receiver.

"Elsa? This is Helen. I don't know if I should have called you about this, but Peg was so upset—"

"Something happen to Peggy?" Elsa said sharply.

"No, no, she's all right. But . . . Elsa, there was another call. From Michael. It came while we were on the way home from Gladden. I don't know where Brenda was—in the cellar, I suppose—and Peg answered."

"She talk to him? You sound—"

"Yes, she talked to him. Elsa, where's Andy?"

"With his bees. Why?"

"Michael told Peggy that . . . bad things are going to happen in The Shades, to friends of ours."

"Ha?" Elsa said, forgetting the steaks.

"And that's why I asked about Andy. Michael said . . . he said that Andy—"

Helen didn't have a chance to finish. Elsa

dropped the receiver to the wall telephone and hurried across her kitchen to peer out the window over the sink. She could see the lights of the apiary barn through the thickened fog, but little of the building itself. For a few moments she stared in dismay, then returned to the telephone.

"Hang up now, I'll call you back," she said brusquely to Helen.

"Is something—"

Elsa cut her off, then quickly dialed the three digits that would ring the telephone in the barn workroom. The ringing went on for a half minute. When no one answered Elsa replaced the receiver, half ran to the back door, knocking over a chair that was in her way.

"Andy!" she cried.

It was not far across the lot to the barn, but the ground sloped and fog obscured her path. Twice she almost fell, and her heart felt as if it were being pulled apart. She was afraid of another coronary but she was more afraid of this last, ominous phone call from Michael. She wanted to see her husband, and she didn't care how much of a fool she would look when she burst in on him.

"Andy?"

The metal door resisted her the first time she tried to open it. Sobbing for breath, Elsa kicked at it, and stepped inside.

In the shadowless mild air she was confronted by a nightmare of swarming bees.

Beside the door, hanging on the wall, was a beekeeper's veil, heavy protective gloves, a full-length coat of heavy denim and a red cylinder like a fire extinguisher which contained insecticide. After several shocking seconds during which she thought her heart must surely fail, Elsa fumbled for the veil, put on the protective clothing and opened the valve of the tank of insecticide.

I will die, she thought, and found herself praying to die, because he hadn't moved.

Poisoned bees leaped up from the tanbark, stinging futilely at her horseman's boots as she walked deeper into the barn. Bees fell like rain against the impenetrable veil, glanced off the denim coat.

He's strong, she thought. *He may survive this . . .* She saw his face, and gave up hope.

Elsa stood over her husband spraying in every direction, until the noxious fog inside the barn was nearly as heavy as the fog outside, until the furious bees were dead, or had retreated. Then she dropped the red cylinder, knelt clumsily, picked her husband up and carried him in her arms to the nearest door. She was forced to put him down long enough to snap the dead bolt back, and when she tried to pick him up again she found her strength was almost gone. So she grasped Andy under the arms and dragged him outside, into the cold air and the cold fog.

Elsa turned, and caught a glimpse of someone standing close.

Help, she said, or thought she said. *Help me.*

And then she saw him more clearly, as if the fog had suddenly dissolved where he stood, silently, looking on, his young round fair face expressionless, his dark eyes sad and inquiring. He seemed to have an air of abandonment about him; he had always looked that way to Elsa.

"Michael!" she screamed, and toppled down beside her husband in a faint.

5

Aron Landers' cousin Chuck was over from Round Spring for the day and, although it was early, he was already making Aron's life miserable, as only Chuck knew how. Chuck was nine, barely two years older than Aron, but he was tall for his age and had the kind of insolence which uncritical children accept as sophistication.

He'd started off by commandeering Aron's bike—which Aron wasn't too good at riding yet—and now he was showing off on it for the benefit of the two girls, Aron's sister Melissa and her friend Carol-Sue. He'd pedal lazily down the gravel road, barely holding on, then come back furiously, jam on the brakes, skid the bike halfway around in the gravel, winding up with a flourish, left foot on the ground, the other carelessly astride the leaning bike. Aron had said, "You'll ruin the tires," and Chuck had said, "Not if they're good tires." Aron was willing then to let him go on until he wrecked the bike and skinned himself, giving double satisfaction, but it wasn't too likely Chuck would goof, and if he did he'd find some way to blame Aron or Aron's bike for the mishap.

It looked like a day impossible to survive without some sort of personal disgrace (he still cried too easily when provoked, the ultimate disgrace with two younger girls looking on) when the possibility of salvation appeared: a fuming, grimy-red motor scooter came chugging down the road at a dead-game twenty miles an hour, carrying a bespectacled man so tall that his knees were nearly at the level of the handle bars as he rode.

"Doremus!" Aron shouted gleefully, and went running toward the oncoming scooter, passing and ignoring Chuck, who was trying to bring the bicycle to a stop with the front wheel in the air.

His motor scooter shuddered pathetically as Doremus Brightlaw slowed and said loudly over the racket of the engine, "Aron; how are you this morning?"

Aron jogged along, keeping half an eye on Chuck, who was turned around on the bicycle seat watching from the middle of the road. Melissa and Carol-Sue, who also knew Doremus, were scampering toward them.

"Are you going to town, Doremus?" Aron asked hopefully.

"I thought I would; see if it's still there." He peered at Chuck, still taking up the road. "Who's that on the bike?" He reached for his klaxon, to Aron's delight, and gave Chuck a couple of honks.

"That's my cousin; he doesn't live around here."

"Hi, Doremus!"

"Hi, Melissa. How's that cat of yours?"

59

"She's still at the vet."

"Been there a long time. Awful sick, is she?"

Chuck continued to stare at the oncoming Doremus with a certain amount of resentment, and then at the last possible instant he pushed Aron's bike to the side of the road.

Aron said, panting, "My dad's downtown, Doremus. He'll run me home if I can ride along with you." He'd seen a few of the older kids hitch rides with Doremus, but he was appalled by his own temerity.

Doremus came to a full stop and frowned as he struggled to keep the engine alive. Then he sneaked a casual glance at Aron. Doremus Brightlaw was in his forties; he had a slightly emaciated look, was comfortably weathered and a little bit gray. When he took off his sunglasses to blow the dust of the road from the lenses, his eyes were a light shade of blue and markedly judicial. He took in Aron and Chuck without appearing to and said, "I was about to ask if you'd like to ride along, Aron. Hop on back there."

When Aron was firmly in place, Doremus drove on. The girls ran along beside the road. Doremus waved but Aron was too thrilled to do anything except cling to Doremus' windbreaker.

"Your cousin looks like he's OK," Doremus yelled as they puttered into the village at fifteen miles an hour.

"Yeah, he's OK," Aron allowed, from the heights of his triumph. He saw a couple of kids he knew in front of Rockwell's Café, but he pretended he didn't see them. He was hoping Doremus might be going clear across to the other side of town, but instead Doremus swung into the parking lot behind the post office.

'Where's your dad now?"

"Oh, he's at the MFA. Doremus, if you're going back before lunch . . ."

Doremus smiled. "No, I'll be a little longer than that, Aron."

"OK." Aron raced off. "I'll see you," he shouted back. "Thanks, Doremus!"

"Come over when you get the time, Aron." Doremus went on into the post office, mailed the once-a-week letter to his sister in Berwyn, Illinois, a suburb of Chicago which he visited dutifully once a year, and then he mailed the once-a-month letter to a man named Vladislav Arshenko, who lived in a suburb of Moscow, a place he'd never laid eyes on and had no desire to visit. Afterward he unloaded his mailbox and went through the accumulated mail leisurely, dropping half of it unopened into the closest wastebasket.

"Might lose out on some big sweepstakes doing that," someone observed.

Doremus glanced up. "Well, you see, it's necessary, Hap. I'm probably one of the world's luckiest men. I mean money's just always stuck to my fingers somehow, and I'm afraid I'd get to winning so many of these things the Treasury Department would set up a branch office in my spare bedroom."

Hap Washbrook leaned against the bank of mailboxes, thumbs hooked over the wide leather belt he wore; because of his girth and the tilt of his Stetson hat, he looked to be a caricature of a county sheriff, all gimme and graft; his bashed and sun-reddened face reinforced the impression. But he was neither dishonest nor a dummy. He'd been a colonel in the Military Police until his retirement from the Army, and his county was annually visited by over a quarter of a million people, including a preponderance of hunters, who brought a lot of guns with them and frequently shot each other, sometimes out of malice. In twenty years Hap had become expert at sorting out the accidental deaths from the suspicious ones, and he knew as much about gunshot wounds as a good medical examiner.

"Now," Hap said thoughtfully, "if I was lucky and won a Cadillac full of cash, I think I'd drive that Caddy down to Acapulco, Mexico. All week I've been thinking about Mexico. You know anything about Acapulco?"

"Not a thing, Hap."

"It's my idea of paradise. Lots of sun, gorgeous women. Of course, I always get like this a few weeks before the deer hunters come in. Give me any other place on earth but Shades County during deer season. Buy you a cup of coffee?"

Doremus agreed and the two men left the post office, walked leisurely down the sidewalk toward the center of the village, past the Little Theater and Weldon's Antiques and the Village Center Art Gallery.

"Haven't seen you around the village last couple of weeks," said Hap. "Occurred to me you might have had some second thoughts about settling down around here."

"Hap, I've been in The Shades two years now, and I look on that as being settled."

"Well, I figured you had a change of heart and threw in with that detective agency's been after you."

Doremus smiled slightly and said nothing.

"Biggest detective agency in the Middle West," Hap mused, pushing open the front door of the

Hartshorn Pharmacy. "Wouldn't mind a deal like that for myself."

"They'd make you wear a tie to work, Hap. Besides, it's dull. Like selling shoes."

"This morning I wish I *was* selling shoes."

They sat down in a booth and Hap signaled a waitress. Doremus glanced a second time at the sheriff's reddened weary eyes and said, "Got yourself a bad one, Hap?"

"Andy Britton died last night. Know him?"

"The doctor? He treated me for frostbite last winter. What happened?"

"Some of his bees stung him to death."

"Honeybees?"

Hap gave Doremus a vexed look. "Didn't know there was any other kind. Anyway, he had about half a million of the bastards in his barn, and they jumped him."

"Just like that?"

"I suppose he got careless handling them." The waitress came with their coffee. "One of those jelly doughnuts too, Dolores," Hap said.

"Had he worked around bees long?"

"Elsa told me Andy'd kept bees as long as she can remember, and they were married thirty-eight years. She's the one found him, and she's got a heart condition. Last night it was touch and go, believe me, but I think Elsa will be all right. Tough old German." He looked down glumly at his steaming coffee. "And being dead is right hard to take. I admired him, but there's more to it than that. Mind listening?"

"Not at all, Hap."

The sheriff explained in a rambling way about the telephone calls Helen Connelly had received from the boy who called himself Michael, sketched the family history of the Youngs and concluded with the glimpse Elsa had had of "Michael himself."

When he was finished Doremus smoked a miniature cigar halfway before saying, "Are you satisfied that bee venom caused Britton's death?"

"From the looks of him I'd be real surprised if it was anything else, but the body's going up to Jeff this afternoon for an autopsy. More coffee?"

"No thanks, Hap. That boy Mrs. Britton saw: could he have been a neighbor?"

"She didn't know him. I mean he wasn't anybody *living*; he was Michael Young as far as Elsa's concerned."

"And the boy who talked to Helen Connelly's daughter predicted Britton's death?"

"I haven't been able to get that straight," Hap admitted. "I went over to Helen Connelly's early this morning to find out what Peggy remembered about the phone call, but she's so upset over Andy she won't talk to anybody. Andy more or less took the place of a father, since she never knew her own father."

"Mrs. Connelly a widow?"

"Her husband was Ed Connelly. Good friend of mine. He was a game warden. Died one spring during a flash flood on the Black Fork. I was wondering, Doremus . . . I really would like to know about the conversation Peggy had with this boy. You've got a knack with the kids which I don't have. If you could spare the time. . . ."

"I've been out of police work awhile, Hap."

"I know. But this ain't exactly police work."

"Well . . . I'll be glad to help you out if I can, Hap. But this little girl—Peggy?—might not want to talk to me either."

* * *

They drove in Hap's unmarked car to the Connellys'; Helen was still at the Britton farm, but Craig and Amy met them on the front porch.

"Doremus used to be with the Chicago police," Hap said after introducing him.

Craig looked a great deal more interested than he had upon shaking hands with Doremus. "Oh, really? What department?"

"I was a detective."

"Homicide," Hap added.

Craig smiled in a complimentary way. "What brings you to The Shades, Mr. Brightlaw? Vacationing?"

"No, I've lived here a couple of years now. Down by Harmony Lake."

"Doremus and I was having some coffee this afternoon and I told him about Andy Britton's death—"

Amy said, "Do you still think it was an accident, Sheriff?"

"I have to think so, until something happens to change my mind, Amy."

"I should think"—Amy met Doremus' blandly inquiring eyes and looked down—"I should think you'd be interested in what Elsa saw last night."

"I'm interested in that boy, but I don't have a clue as to who he might be. I'm also interested in the phone calls, which is why I brought Doremus along. He might be able to talk to Peg."

"Well, I doubt it," Craig told the sheriff. "I've been trying all morning to coax her down from that tree house."

"Tree house," Doremus repeated. "Where is it?"

"Out in the backyard, in the tulip tree next to the garage. I'll show you—"

"Oh, I'll find it," Doremus said, and sauntered off, hands in the pockets of his windbreaker.

Amy looked at Craig, who grinned. "Makes himself right at home," Craig said, as soon as Doremus was beyond hearing.

"I've seen him before, down in the village," Amy mused. "So he used to be a detective. Sort of thin, but still he's very nice looking. I wonder if Helen will be back in time to meet him."

Doremus reached the tulip tree and walked leisurely around the trunk, looking up at the tree house; leaves crackled under his feet.

"Hey!" he said, after a while, then took off his sunglasses, wiped the lenses on his flannel shirt and listened. He searched his pockets for a stick of cinnamon gum, unwrapped it, chewed thoughtfully and studied the ladder nailed to the tree. Then he began to climb, carefully, the rungs of the ladder creaking under him.

The entrance to the tree house was child-sized, barely wide enough for Doremus to squeeze his shoulders through. He stopped climbing and put his weight on his elbows and looked around, seeing Peggy sitting in one sunlit corner with hostility in her eyes. He paid almost no attention to her but continued to admire the tree house.

"This is all right," he said, squinting. "A little small. When I build my tree house I'll want the roof higher. Ought to be enough room for my dog, too. He spends so much time in trees I think he should have a roof over his head. What do you think?"

Peggy was silent for a half minute, and then she said in a neutral voice, "Dogs can't climb trees."

"Some dogs can't climb some trees."

Peggy considered this, and then explained the absence of a dog in her tree house by saying, "My dog was run over."

"I'm sorry to hear that."

Peggy looked out the window beside her head. "He wasn't a good dog," she said, with a heavy heart. "He bit."

"Dogs don't always mean to bite."

"He bit though. Does your dog bite?"

"He's too old."

"I've got . . . an old cat."

"I never had a cat."

"And she's . . . a bad cat. She scratches."

"Cats don't always mean to scratch," Doremus said. "Bees don't always mean to sting either."

"Yes . . . they do," Peggy said, tears running down her cheeks. "I hate bees!"

"Sometimes, Peggy—once in a great while—men who work around bees, like the doctor, get stung, and sometimes they die. Nobody knows for sure why it happens."

Peggy sobbed. "Michael made it happen!" She wanted to go ahead and cry, but the presence of Doremus inhibited her, so she wiped furiously at her eyes, her mouth a thin white line.

"Did he tell you he'd make it happen, Peggy? Did he say the bees were going to sting Dr. Britton?"

"He said . . . bad things were going to happen. He said A-Andy was going to . . . get hurt. It's Michael's fault, he did it! I hate Michael!"

"Do you know him very well?" Doremus asked calmly, not pressing Peggy but giving her enough to think about to keep her from turning away in a brooding silence.

"No."

"I know a boy named Michael Landers—Aron's big brother. Do you know Mike?"

"Yes. He's twelve."

"That's right, he is. But that wasn't who you talked to yesterday."

"No. It was Michael Young."

"Did he tell you that himself?"

"He said . . . his name was Michael, and he said he talked to my mother. I knew who he was."

"But you never talked to him before."

"I saw him once. On the playground. He ran away."

"He didn't talk to you then?" asked Doremus.

"He just . . . ran away."

"I'd like to see him sometime myself," Doremus said. "Would you tell him that if you ever talk to him again?"

"I don't . . . *ever* want to talk to him again," Peggy said, shaking her head.

"He's just a little boy, Peggy. And he can't hurt anybody, not really. And maybe he didn't mean to scare you. It's not much fun when you're all by yourself."

"Is he all by himself?"

"Whoever he is, I think he's awfully lonely."

"Do you think he's dead?"

"No, I don't, Peggy."

Peggy was affected by his certainty. "Mother showed me his picture," she said, but she seemed tired of the subject of Michael. Her eyes were dry again. "Are you going to build a tree house?" she asked Doremus.

"I've been seriously thinking about it."

"Where do you live?"

"At Harmony Lake. Know where that is?"

Peggy nodded. "Craig and Amy took me swimming there this summer."

"You probably saw my house. My name's Doremus. Do-re-mus."

"Do-re-mus," Peggy pronounced, meticulously.

"Would your mother give me a drink of water if I ask her?"

"Yes. But she might not be there. She went to—"

"That's OK, I'll just help myself if you won't show me."

"Oh, I'll show you," Peggy said promptly. She got up and came over to the opening in the floor of the tree house. "You have to be careful going down," she cautioned. "I fell once. Mother wouldn't let me come up here for a week."

When they were both on the ground they walked together to the back porch. "There's Mother," Peggy said delightedly, breaking into a run, and Helen Connelly came outside, wearing a neat black wool dress, unadorned.

"Hi, honey," Helen said, bending to kiss her daughter. She looked then at Doremus with a non-committal smile. He observed that she was quite a bit older than she had looked from a distance. There were sun crinkles and stripes at the throat, but her hair was a rich sun-glossy brown and she had the good legs of a particularly well-favored girl of twenty.

"He wants a drink of water," Peggy said.

"Good morning, Mrs. Connelly. I'm Doremus Brightlaw."

"How do you do, Mr. Brightlaw. Would you like to come in? The others are in the kitchen."

After Peggy had had a glass of milk, Helen coaxed her upstairs to take a bath and returned to find Doremus discussing the meaning of the "Michael" telephone calls with Craig.

Doremus said, "Mrs. Britton saw a young boy resembling the Michael Young she knew, and Peggy saw a boy she believes is Michael. But both of these occurrences might be unrelated to the calls, which in turn are not necessarily related to the death of Dr. Britton."

"How can you say that?" Amy responded indignantly. "Yesterday that boy as much as promised Andy would be killed, and less than an hour later he turns up at the barn where Andy had been stung to death by bees!"

"So far," Hap said, "there's only Elsa's testimony that a boy was there, and she was—well, she was almost hysterical; no telling what she actually saw. Probably some kid taking a shortcut home through the barn lot."

"I believe Elsa," Amy said more quietly. "It may have been an apparition, but she saw Michael."

Craig shook his head wearily. "Ghosts again."

Helen held out a small photograph to Doremus. "I thought you might be interested in seeing this, Mr. Brightlaw. It's a school picture of Michael Young, taken just a couple of months before he died."

Doremus accepted the photo and studied it closely, then passed it on to Hap. Amy and Craig looked over his shoulder.

Craig's expression was bleak. Amy glanced at him sympathetically, seeming a little sorry for her talk about apparitions.

"He looks a lot like the middle Boyer kid," Hap murmured. "A little thinner, maybe."

"There's something about that age," said Craig. "Several of our kids . . ." He shrugged.

"Are the Greenleaf boys under constant supervision?" Doremus asked.

"No, we'd be defeating our purpose. But if that had been a Greenleaf boy Elsa saw last night, I'd know it. He would have had something like a twenty-mile hike, round trip, which means he would have missed an eight-thirty room check."

"Unless, of course, he hitched a ride with somebody."

"Well, that's a possibility," Craig said politely, and Doremus smiled.

Hap rose from the kitchen table. "Helen, I'd like to keep this picture for a while if you don't mind. Show it around."

"Will Elsa have to see it?" Amy asked.

"I'm afraid so."

"Oh, Hap," Helen said glumly.

"Doremus, care to ride along with me to the Britton place?" Hap said, and Doremus surprised him by assenting.

Helen accompanied the two men to the front door, where she said, "Mr. Brightlaw, I appreciate the tact with which you handled Peggy."

Doremus seemed mildly embarrassed. "Peggy's not hard to talk to, Mrs. Connelly. I like her."

Helen said, with a hint of depression in her gray eyes, "Are you going to help us? Hap told me you were a detective at one time."

"That's right. I don't know if there's anything I can do though."

"Michael's going to call again, I'm sure of that."

"If he does," said Hap, "I want you to get in touch with me no matter what hour of the day or night." He frowned. "Wish you'd called me the first time."

When they were in the sheriff's car and on the

way to the Britton farm, Hap said to Doremus, "That's a mighty lot of woman back there."

"Does she do well with that antique shop?"

"Not bad, considering the location. The Weldons do better, and so does Wilhelmina Carley, but they'll sell any kind of trash." Hap scratched his stomach and grinned. "Yeah, I tried to get started with Helen back two—three years ago. Nothing came of it, but then I'm just an old Shades County boy and she's got a lot of background." He slanted a look at Doremus.

"Like to hear about her sometime," Doremus said pleasantly as he smoked his cigar, but he was staring out the window and he seemed to be somewhat bored. He had nothing more to say until they reached the farm. There Hap pointed out the barn in which Dr. Britton had been stung to death, and Doremus perked up.

"OK if I poke around inside, Hap?"

"Sure, the barn's not padlocked. Need to spend a few minutes with old Elsa. There's still plenty of bees inside, so watch yourself."

"Tell me one thing, Hap. Where was the doctor when the bees attacked him?"

"Inside his workroom. You'll see it."

Doremus nodded, got out of the car and headed for the barn, pausing to stomp out his cigar on the way.

For more than a minute after entering, he stood by the door studying the layout of the apiary, and then he proceeded slowly across the tanbark in the artificial brightness to the place, marked with stakes and string, where Andrew Britton had fallen. He looked at the discarded insecticide tank, then took a pocket knife from his trousers and, hunkered down, began prying carefully with the blade in the packed-down tanbark. He exhumed one of the dead bees, held it up on the blade to the level of his eyes and squinted at it. With his other hand he reached into his shirt pocket, slipped the cellophane off the package of cigars he carried there and dropped the bee into this makeshift bag. With the bee stowed away, he went all around the staked area, occasionally squatting to pick up more bees with the knife.

When he was satisfied he straightened up, his stiffened knees popping, and walked across the barn to the row of hives there. Without hesitating, he gently opened one of the hives and peered inside at the combs and the bees clustered there. Then he moved down the row and chose another hive.

Once he had looked into five different hives he turned and went quickly to the prefab building which Dr. Britton had used as a workroom. The door in the side of the rectangular slope-roofed building was standing open. Doremus approached with care and saw the broken hive on the floor near the table, its lid completely off, and he heard the faint buzzing of what was left of the bee colony. He sniffed deeply, aware of the lingering acrid odor of insecticide that had apparently permeated the air of the barn and ultimately killed innocent as well as guilty bees. Then he stepped into the workroom, making sure the door behind him was standing wide. He was also careful to keep a good six feet away from the cracked-open nearly ruined hive, which the survivors undoubtedly were recolonizing.

He made a survey of the bottles and jars on the shelves over the worktable, then noted the jars of paint on the table itself, and what looked like a

discarded surgeon's mask. That brought a frown.
For several minutes he was motionless, thinking.
Finally he squatted down and saw a bottle with a
spray attachment that had rolled partway under
one section of the shelves. He reached for it and
read the label: *Chloroform.*

Automatically he held the bottle close to his
nose and sniffed twice.

He was so puzzled by the contradictory odor
from the amber "chloroform" bottle that he almost sprayed some of the liquid on his hand, but
instinct warned him not to. He turned for another
lingering look at the hive on the floor, then rose
and placed the bottle on the table.

"Anything wrong with that?" Doremus was
asked.

He looked around quickly. Harry Randle was
standing just outside the workroom.

"Found it on the floor," Doremus said amiably.
"Who are you?"

"Randle. I work for the Brittons."

"I didn't see you come in."

Harry jerked his head toward the back door,
which was standing open. "You from the State Patrol?"

Doremus only smiled and left the workroom,
having decided to go out by way of the back door.
Randle followed him leisurely. Outside, the
ground was rocky for a distance of about ten feet,
then there was a slope covered with frostbitten
weed, some bright hawthorn and a couple of Chi-
nese elms growing near the trim white-painted
fence beside the road.

Doremus got out another cigar, lighted it,
pinched the match and dropped it into a handy
pocket. "How about that back door?" he asked

Randle. "Do you know if the doctor usually kept it locked?"

Harry's eyes were steady on Doremus' face. "No idea," he said with a light shrug. "I don't come down here much."

"Don't care for the bees?"

"They never bother me. You working with the sheriff, then?"

"In a way. Did you happen to see the doctor yesterday afternoon, before he died?"

Harry nodded. "We were stacking those bales of hay you saw inside. Finished about dark. I took the truck down to Claypool's. The bees must have got him right after I left."

Doremus pondered this. "Did you notice any unusual activity while you were in the barn?"

"You mean the bees? There were a few around. The doctor said that was normal. He said they wouldn't swarm unless they were ... interfered with. Stirred up. I guess he stirred them up some way. Well, I'd better get that rake I was after." He turned back to the barn.

"Please don't touch anything inside if you can avoid it."

"Why would I do that? Should I fix the lock on the door when I leave?"

"Might be a good idea." Doremus strolled around the barn to Hap's car. The sheriff had come down from the house and was talking by radio to his office.

"Any problems with the bees?" Hap said, after he'd replaced the radio microphone.

"No." Doremus produced the cellophane sack he'd made. "I borrowed one, if you don't mind."

Hap grimaced. "Take 'em all. Old Elsa's going to have the lot burned anyhow."

"Is she? That's a shame. Looks as if the only German bees the doctor had were the ones that took after him. I suppose these are the U.S. variety of Germans, and not imported. There are a couple of nice colonies of Italian bees in there, and two hives of Caucasians. Both fine breeds, and not excitable. Cyprian bees are probably nastier than the Germans, but they're yellow. I didn't notice any dead yellow bees around the spot where he died."

The sheriff smiled a lopsided, admiring smile. "So you're a bee expert."

"Not at all. My Uncle Swen keeps bees on his farm in Wisconsin, but I've forgot half of what I ever learned from him. Believe I'll give him a call."

"Find out something interesting?" Hap said quickly.

"Can't say that I did, but I'd like to know what would make those German bees swarm so suddenly that an experienced beekeeper would panic. He was just a few feet from the door, and safety, and he'd been bitten before, I'm sure. I think maybe a couple of hundred of them stung him at once."

"Even an autopsy couldn't determine that. Is it unusual?"

"Damned unusual." Doremus put his dead bee back in a pocket of the windbreaker and stood smoking and gazing at the blue sky. Hap nibbled at a thumbnail.

"This *was* an accident, wasn't it, Doremus?"

"I don't think Britton was a fool, and he was sure to be cautious around an open hive of German bees. Yet they swarmed on him. Well, maybe that's an act of God or something. How often was he down here, Hap? Two or three days a week?"

"More often than that. I'd say nearly every afternoon."

"So if I wanted the doctor for something, I could count on finding him around his apiary late in the day?"

Hap nodded. "What are you thinking about, Doremus?"

"I'm wondering if he had company just before he died, other than Harry Randle."

"I've talked to everybody who was on the place at the time. Except for Randle, the hands are scared of the bees; the stay well away from here. All right, what if he *did* have company?"

Instead of replying, Doremus asked, "Did you show that photograph to Mrs. Britton?"

"Yehp. She'll swear on a Bible she was looking at Michael Young. There was fog, she says, but she saw him clear as day. Can you beat that?" He blinked his reddened eyes and looked hard at Doremus. "*Now* what are you thinking?"

"I think it's possible there was a ghost inside the barn before the bees swarmed and killed the doctor," Doremus said, looking perfectly serious.

"I'll be . . ." Hap started, and dried up, and then said, with some seriousness, "You a ghost expert too, Doremus?"

"No. But I have an aunt in Indiana who's gotten a rise out of a few spirits. Maybe I'll give her a call."

"God damn it, Doremus—"

Doremus gave him a level look. "If it wasn't a ghost, then I have to believe in the possibility of a nine- or ten-year-old homicidal maniac. That possibility freezes my blood. Those bees were made to swarm, Hap. I'm not sure how yet, but I think I can find out if you want me to."

"He was murdered?"

"That's the tricky part. I don't think murder could ever be proved."

"God damn it," the sheriff said despairingly. "What are we in for?"

"Well, it's still awhile to deer season, Hap, and you weren't doing anything anyway."

6

Doremus owned several wooded acres and a small house built on a mighty slab of limestone overlooking a wide stretch of the spring-fed Competition River; the half-mile-long part of the river was not deep enough to be called a lake but here the often turbulent river slowed and eddied peacefully much of the year, turning a deep green color, and so someone a long time ago had tagged the place Harmony Lake. Not far from Doremus' front porch there was a waterfall that twined and trickled down the rock surface to the water, and enough sun penetrated the brassy autumn foliage to keep his house from growing damp and musty.

The house had been in terrible shape when he'd moved in and he'd spent most of one winter learning the roofer's trade, a feat for a man who'd never held a hammer before. He was now a reasonably skilled carpenter who tackled ambitious projects—an extra room, a rebuilt front porch—with success.

Most of Saturday afternoon following his visit to the Britton farm he spent on his hands and knees nailing porch flooring in place, watched over by three railbirds named Tim, Maisy and Seth, who handed down tools or nails when he asked for them and managed to stay out of his way.

The telephone inside the house rang for what seemed like the tenth time that afternoon.

Maisy turned to Tim, who beat her to the punch by saying vehemently, "It's *your* mother!"

"It is not!"

"Somebody answer that," Doremus said patiently.

Seth, with a superior look, said to Maisy, "She thinks you fell in the lake by now."

"I went last time," Tim grumbled.

Doremus pounded another nail. "I'm expecting a long-distance call," he said.

The three railbirds were silent and acted stone deaf. Each was afraid that it might be his mother after all, and he would have to go home.

"OK," Doremus said with a sigh, and he got up creakingly.

The caller wasn't his Uncle Swen in Wisconsin; it was Helen Connelly.

"Mr. Brightlaw, I'm terribly embarrassed to call, but you were so nice to Peggy this morning that I wonder if—" She lost her voice momentarily, then continued in a rush, "Peg's not there with you, is she?"

"No, I haven't seen her since I left your house, Mrs. Connelly. Is she missing?"

"I'm . . . afraid so. I drove Peg to the Methodist Church early this afternoon with several of the other neighborhood children to rehearse for the reunion—the whole thing was going to be called off, but Elsa heard and said no, Andy wouldn't have wanted it that way. Well, I left the children at the church and went on to Elsa's. I had intended to stay about an hour, but once I got there I felt I just couldn't leave right away, and then when I reached home a little while ago Peggy wasn't here. One of the mothers was supposed to drive her home but there'd been a lot of confusion at the church, of course, with a hundred boys and girls—"

"Peggy doesn't have another hideout, does she?"

"I beg your pardon?"

"Other than the tree house."

"I see what you mean. No, only the tree house. I called everyone I could think of, but Peggy's not visiting any of her usual friends. Then I tried the church, and Reverend Bartlett remembered seeing her with Maisy Duncan, and that's how the whole thing has gotten around to you." Helen laughed, but clearly she was worried. "Peg's not a thoughtless child, and she's not given to wandering off—"

"Let me see what Maisy has to say," Doremus suggested, and called the little girl into the kitchen. "Did you talk to Peggy Connelly today?" he asked her.

Maisy nodded. "At the church."

"Did Peggy ride home with you?"

"No, sir."

"Did your mother bring you home?"

"No, sir."

"Who did?"

"I forget."

"Could you try to remember?"

81

Maisy made a stab at concentration, her eyes on the ceiling. "Mrs. Cummings."

"Did Peggy tell you where she was going to be this afternoon?" Maisy shook her head. "OK," Doremus said. "There's root beer in the icebox. Would you help yourself and give a couple to the boys?" Doremus repeated what Maisy had told him for Helen's benefit.

"I'll just have to get in the car and go looking. I'm sorry again for—"

"Excuse me, Mrs. Connelly . . . What was that, Maisy?"

Blond Maisy was on tiptoe, reaching into the refrigerator. "Said she was going to look for Michael."

"Peggy said that? Why didn't you tell me before?"

Maisy shrugged and carefully set another bottle of root beer on the floor.

Doremus glanced at his wristwatch. It was five minutes past four. His hand was covering the speaker of the telephone receiver. "Michael who?" he asked.

"Wellll . . . *I* don't know."

"The opener's right there on the cabinet, Maisy." Doremus looked dubiously at the receiver in his hand and then said to Helen, "Maisy remembers now that Peggy mentioned something about going to look for Michael."

After a two-second hesitation Helen said in a low voice, "Dear God."

"Mrs. Connelly, I'd like to help you look for Peggy, unless you have some other ideas about where she might be."

"I don't, no. Should I call the sheriff?"

Doremus responded to her hint of fear by saying, "I doubt that'll be necessary." He glanced at Maisy, who was prying the caps off the bottles of root beer. "Right now I have company," he told Helen, "and it will be about ten minutes before I can start them home. If you wouldn't mind driving down this way . . ."

"Not at all," Helen said instantly.

"Good. I'm at the end of Competition Road, where it turns to gravel."

By the time Helen Connelly reached Doremus' house the sun was low in the trees, its light clear but remote, and where Doremus stood waiting the porch was dark.

Helen said when they were under way, "I don't understand what would compel Peg to go off on her own—she isn't that adventurous. She must still be very upset with Mi—with whoever-he-is. I explained to her as carefully as I could that Michael Young died many years ago, but of course she talked to 'Michael' on the telephone, so he seems as real as any of the boys she knows." Helen smiled tensely. "He seems real to me."

"Where is the Methodist Church, Mrs. Connelly? Almost in the village, isn't it?"

"Yes, it's at the corner of Scotia and Pine."

"Did Peggy have any money with her?"

"I think she had about twenty cents in her purse."

"Chances are she got as far as the village center, then decided to have a soda. Now she's wondering how to get home."

Helen, who was ready for any agreeable explanation of Peggy's absence, said ruefully, "I must be losing my mother's instinct. That's what she's done. I'll bet she's in Huffaker's right now, talking Charley's ear off. Charley was her summer's love—

he's fifteen, and he taught her to swim." Helen slowed for a stop sign. The sky in the east was darkening from rain clouds. "I'm afraid I've wasted quite a lot of your time, Mr. Brightlaw. There's no point in your riding all the way to the village with me if you'd rather—"

"It's no waste of time. And, uh, if you don't mind—uh, Doremus?"

"If I can stop being Mrs. Connelly."

He smiled fitfully, and Helen made a small discovery: earlier he had seemed preoccupied, even obtuse to her, but in fact his manner was due to shyness, or—she changed her mind again—timidity. An unusual trait for a policeman, or ex-policeman, Helen thought. He seemed young to be retired. Perhaps he hadn't been very good with people, and consequently not good at his job. But, no, Hap Washbrook had seemed almost in awe of him, and Hap customarily deferred to no man.

"If I may say so, you know a great deal about children and their ways, Doremus. Do you have children of your own?"

"No. My sister has quite a brood though. So Marian and I sort of borrowed her kids from time to time."

"You're married then?"

"Was married. Say, do you mind if I smoke a cigar?"

Helen didn't mind, and once Doremus had his cigar going he lost a certain amount of his reserve, or timidity, or whatever it was, and seemed more at home with her. The sun was setting, filling the inside of the car with a golden light; the storm clouds ahead were dark blue and resembled a vast mountain range dwarfing the ridges and hills of the land of The Shades.

Helen double-parked in front of Huffaker's sandwich shop and went in, but she was back quickly, shaking her head. "Charley hasn't seen her today. Let's see . . . the variety store is closed, but there are two other places Peg likes to visit."

They drove across long-unused railroad tracks to the south edge of town and the local Dairy Dreme, but Peg wasn't there either, they could see that without leaving the car; and she wasn't in Coyles' bakery watching the hot bread loaves come off the line.

"I'll call home," Helen said, but she got only Brenda, who reported that Peggy had neither "showed her face" nor called.

When Helen returned to the ranch wagon the sky was two-thirds dark, and Doremus was starting his second cigar. For half a minute Helen sat with her hands on the wheel, not knowing where to go, and then she said, giving up all pretense of good cheer, "This is beginning to scare me. It's ten after five."

"Chances are she's with a friend," Doremus said calmly. "Dinnertime will come before long and Peggy'll remember she has a home. It might be best if you went back to your house, because she's bound to call. You can leave me at the Trailways depot; the six-o'clock bus to Polar Bluff will drop me off five minutes from my place."

"I wouldn't think of doing that," Helen said automatically, staring at the lighted telephone booth she had just left. Her skin looked preternaturally white under the sodium-vapor parking-lot lamp and her curled lip seemed frozen, sickened. She said, with an audible intake of breath, "What I'm afraid of now . . . She wanted to find Michael. Instead he found her. Again. And this time he didn't run away."

Doremus turned his head sharply. "Would you tell me that again?"

"When I showed Peggy Michael Young's school photo—the same one I gave to the sheriff—she said, 'Oh, yes, I've seen him.' And when I asked her where—" Helen broke off, looking astonished. "*That's* where she is! She saw this boy she believes is Michael on the school playground two or three weeks ago. As far as Peggy is concerned, that's the place to look for him again."

The Shades consolidated school, located directly under Constable Ridge, was less than half a mile away along the same road they were on. There were asphalt parking lots on both sides of the four-building complex and playing fields behind it. The front of the school and the parking lots were well lighted. Helen made a single sweep around the school, but neither of them saw Peggy. She then stopped behind the cafeteria and Doremus got out, looking across the playing fields to the black rise of the heavily wooded ridge.

"I see somebody," he said. "Honk your horn." Helen leaned on the horn and also rolled down her window and called.

Presently Peggy came running through the gloom and arrived out of breath and red in the face. Helen was both angry and concerned at the sight of her daughter.

"I've been searching for you," she snapped. "All over."

Peggy looked at Doremus and then at her mother, and said nothing.

"Well, get in the car," Helen said.

"I'm sorry you're mad."

"I'm sorry you've made me mad."

"I wanted to see Michael," Peggy explained, in a low voice.

"Peggy—" Helen started ominously, but Doremus cut her off.

"Did you see him?"

Peggy eyed Doremus again, and decided she had an ally. "No. He lives in the woods. But he didn't come out today. I wanted to tell him"—Peggy's mouth turned down and her face looked redder than before—"I wanted to tell him to leave us alone, and not . . . not hurt anybody else. Like he hurt Andy." She lowered her eyes and stood looking miserably at the ground.

"Baby," Helen said, more gently, "please get in the car now."

"I don't want to . . . if you're going to be mad at me."

"I'm not mad anymore. We'll just forget about the whole thing. And we'll forget about Michael too."

Peggy was struggling not to cry.

"I called Brenda, and she said we were having chicken dumplings for supper. Maybe if you ask Doremus, he'll stay and eat with us."

Peggy wiped her eyes and forgot her unhappiness at the prospect of company. "Do you want to stay?" she said to Doremus.

"There's only one thing I like better than chicken dumplings," Doremus replied.

"What?"

Doremus took the cigar from his mouth, studied the ash in a perplexed way, then hunched his shoulders and shook his head. "I forget," he said.

Peggy smiled a tiny smile, and they all got into the ranch wagon, Peggy in the middle where she could dial the radio. She found a station playing hillbilly music and settled back to enjoy it.

Over the din Doremus said to Helen, "What's on the other side of that ridge? It's on the way to the Greenleaf School, isn't it?"

"Yes. I'd say Greenleaf is about two miles beyond the ridge, possibly a little less."

"Not too long a walk for a ten-year-old boy with an itch to travel," Doremus murmured, but Peggy had turned the volume on the radio up, and Helen couldn't hear him.

After supper Peggy amused Doremus by showing off her favorite antiques while Helen did the dishes. Peggy's favorites numbered in the hundreds and she could talk about them almost as well as her mother could, but Doremus' interest and patience never seemed to waver. Helen didn't know if he cared for antiques, and ordinarily she would have called Peggy off after a few minutes to give him a rest; however, she had a notion that Doremus would have been as disappointed by this as Peggy. Helen was eager to talk to him about the "Michael" mystery, but she decided to wait until after he completed the long-distance call which earlier he'd asked to make.

Outside, the rain had begun to come down heavily but peacefully, without wind or thunder. Helen had a second cup of coffee in the kitchen after loading her dishwasher and then went in search of her guest, who was sitting on a horsehair settee in what had been the parlor of the house, cigar smoke curling around his head, while Peggy explained the purpose of a Georgian silver pap dish.

"Doremus has a telephone call to make while you put all those things back," Helen said.

"Then I think I'd better be on my way."

"The telephone's in the hall," Helen explained, as Doremus accompanied her. "But I can move it to my office without any trouble—"

"That isn't necessary. I just want to give my Uncle Swen a ring and ask him a couple of questions about bees."

"Oh," Helen said. "About bees?" She was about to return to the parlor to help Peggy straighten up but Doremus motioned for her to stay. He sat down on the steps with the telephone in his lap, balanced his lighted cigar on the toe of one shoe and put through his call to Wisconsin.

"Uncle Swen? This is Doremus. . . . Yehp, Doremus. . . . No, I'm not in Chicago, I'm down here in . . . Well, they're all fine far as I know, all seven of 'em. . . . You didn't hear? No, there's seven now; I'm sure they must have sent you an announcement. Karl fell out of a tree this summer and broke his arm. . . . That was *last* summer, this time it was his arm, but not his pitching arm. Uncle Swen, what I called about, there was a man down here stung to death by bees yesterday, and . . . German bees, Swen. . . . Yehp, that's exactly the way I'd describe them. . . . No, he knew what he was doing; he'd handled bees for years. This was indoors, and he was using what he thought was chloroform on the colony before he removed some of the bees for experimental purposes. Only I don't think it *was* chloroform; it had a different odor. Like ripe bananas."

Doremus picked up his cigar and clamped it into his mouth, and he listened without uttering a sound for what seemed like five minutes to Helen, and as he listened, new, hard lines came into his face and he looked like a different man. She couldn't help shuddering as the rain roared down on the roof.

"All right, Swen, thanks for the information. One more thing: what sort of effect would a ghost have on a hive full of bees?" Doremus grinned suddenly and held the receiver of the telephone slightly away from his ear so Helen could hear the hoarse laughter of Uncle Swen in Wisconsin.

When he could get a word in, Doremus said, "Just a little blackberry cordial after supper, Swen. Thanks again for the information; I'll let you know all about it one of these days. . . . No, I'm still retired. Just sort of poking around the edges of what might be a murder case."

He hung up, still grinning, but when he saw Helen's shocked face he looked bleak and sorry for his slip of the tongue.

"How could Andy have been murdered?" Helen asked quietly, looking to see that Peg was nowhere around.

"I'm not sure," Doremus said hastily. "But I have a clear idea now of what happened to him. He thought he was spraying a solution of chloroform into the opened hive, but the contents of the bottle was something else altogether: an essence of bee venom, strong enough to provoke bees into suicidal rage. A honeybee can only sting once, you know, and then it dies, and bees seem to realize this, so nearly all varieties will put up with a heck of a lot before committing themselves to a sting and death. On the other hand, even the best-natured bees will swarm and sting occasionally for mysterious reasons. As far as my Uncle Swen knows, all bees react violently to the odor of venom. A couple of times he's had to burn those elbow-length gloves beekeepers sometimes wear because the gloves have become saturated with bee venom, and to handle a hive while wearing them might bring on an attack."

"Andy must have made a mistake and used the wrong bottle," Helen said.

"That's entirely possible. The bottle was labeled chloroform, but there were many brown and amber bottles on his workroom shelves, some labeled, some not. Undoubtedly one of those contains chloroform. I'll find that out in the morning." Doremus decided his cigar was becoming rank and put it out in a nearby ashtray. "I'm sorry I used the word *murder*; it's unjustified. Conceivably someone who knew a great deal about Dr. Britton's hobby and afternoon schedule, and quite a lot about bees as well, could have switched labels on two bottles of chloroform and bee venom, which would be as effective as putting a shotgun to the doctor's head, and much safer. It's also conceivable that one of the hands on the Britton farm, sent into the workroom for some purpose or other, got panicky or in too much of a hurry because of the nearness of all those bees, knocked several bottles from the shelves and then in confusion mislabeled them. I'd want a chemist or pharmacist to check the contents of every bottle in that workroom, to make sure the contents matched the label. I suppose Hap can have someone do that."

"What if only the venom bottle was mislabeled?"

"Then I'd be inclined to think that it was done on purpose."

Helen looked for a chair, sat down, hands joined in her lap. "By a—by who? And why? Andy Britton was—I can't believe anyone could dislike him enough to cause his death in such a horrible way."

"I'd look for simple motives. A long-held grudge, for instance. How old was the doctor? About sixty-five? Probably that rules out women"—Helen looked offended—"but not inevitably." Doremus put the telephone back on the Sheraton table and walked to the front door, stood gazing out at the planetary street light through a waxen shower of rain. "I'd look for simple motives, but there's the problem of Michael. Who is he, and what does he know? What do *we* know about him? As your nephew Craig says, he's a boy with an amazingly inventive mind, what appears to be an endless capacity for fantasy, and at least a touch of evil. He also has a capacity for getting around—and it's almost too good to be true that Mrs. Britton should happen across him as she's dragging her dead husband from the barn." Doremus pondered his suppositions. "Chances are we're dealing with as many as three boys, all about the same age, linked together by coincidence alone. Or else we're involved with the supernatural, as Miss Lawlor seems to think, but that offends good sense and makes any kind of logical detective work impossible."

Doremus turned to look at Helen, and his expression became less severe. "Tell me about Michael Young," he said. "How long was he missing before his body was found?"

"There wasn't . . . a body. Just clothing, and bones. I believe it was seven months altogether before berrypickers discovered the remains, in a gully where he'd fallen."

"How was he identified? By dental charts?"

"No. I recognized the plaid coat he'd had on the night he disappeared. That seemed to be . . . enough."

"He'd be about twenty-six today, wouldn't he?"

"Yes," Helen said.

"If he were alive," Doremus said—and Helen came halfway up out of her chair—"if Michael Young were alive after all, then some of our questions would be answered. But that possibility offends good sense too—" He caught sight of Helen again and seemed surprised and chagrined by her reaction. "Sorry, I have this habit of thinking out loud. Say, it's almost eight-thirty; you must be ready to throw me out by now."

Helen protested, but truthfully she felt the beginnings of a headache and a less definite sense of distress, caused by his presence. Not because she found Doremus difficult to like—he was a little strange but entertaining and always pleasant. Helen objected most to his detachment in discussing Andy's death, in the casual way he treated the whole terrifying sequence of events as an elaborate puzzle contrived for his entertainment. He seemed to forget that she had been very close to Andy, and that she was still anguished about his death, often close to tears, no matter what sort of effort she made for Peggy's sake.

She wanted very much to be alone and so she protested badly, and Doremus was aware of it; they had nothing to say to each other while Peggy ran upstairs for her own and her mother's coat. Doremus watched the rain come down and retreated into remoteness behind a cigar and Helen simply waited, enduring the wait and the rain and the prospect of a long drive. It was a depressing end for what had been a lively evening.

7

The rain had stopped completely by the time Helen was on the road back from Doremus' house, with Peggy asleep beside her on the front seat. The air was still and wet and chilly and the moon was trying to come out, but Helen didn't see the black overflow from the little river in the hollow until she rounded a bend and plunged down into it at thirty-five miles an hour.

Wings of water drenched the windshield but she didn't panic and, relying on memory, she kept the ranch wagon on the road until she was out of the hollow and the overflow, at which time she recovered sufficiently from shock to start trembling, knowing that if they had veered off the road into the river itself they probably would have drowned.

At the top of the next rise Helen pulled over and stopped for a few moments to regain her composure, and while she was sitting there the lights flickered and dimmed and she discovered that the engine had died.

She glanced at Peggy, who unaccountably had slept through the explosion of car into water and who continued to sleep blissfully with her hands clasped under one cheek. But it had been a long, trying day for Peggy. Helen sighed and wished they were home and tried to start the engine.

After the fourth try she succeeded in killing the lights altogether. Helen knew nothing about automobiles, but she knew that they needed electricity to run, and that undoubtedly there were wires somewhere which must be soaking wet from the overflowing river. So she and Peggy would go nowhere until a car came by.

In the meantime they were alone in the dark without lights or heat. The moon had broken through high clouds and her surroundings were visible, but Helen didn't need the moon to know exactly where she was, and she was aware of how seldom anyone traveled that particular road after dark. She then began to worry that someone *would* come, from the direction in which she had come but at a higher speed, and have an accident. Hap should know about the overflow, Helen decided, and she felt sure he would send a car for her.

She opened the door and got out, taking care not to disturb Peg. There were three mailboxes a few feet from where she had parked, and a gravel road angled up the ridge above her. It was so quiet she could hear rain dripping from the leaves in the woods.

Three houses on the ridge, Helen thought. But one had burned more than sixteen years ago, and was abandoned; she would not go there. A family named Kutner owned a house about halfway up the road, a distance of perhaps two hundred yards, but Helen could not remember if they were summer people. She told herself that if no one was at home she would not mind breaking in to use the telephone; otherwise she would have to take Peg and walk more than a mile down the dark country road to a point where it intersected Route 22.

Helen turned and looked through the closed window at her sleeping daughter, then decided to lock both doors. Her footsteps sounded unnaturally loud to her as she walked around the ranch wagon to Peg's side and turned the key in the door lock. It worried her to leave Peggy alone even for ten minutes, but the wagon was pulled well off the blacktop, and probably nothing would happen to disturb her daughter's sleep.

With the doors locked, Helen walked quietly up the rutted and rain-slicked road, finding her way by the moon. The wood lot to her left was filled with a light luminous mist and looked beautiful in a desolate way. On her right was a crowding woods, impenetrable; it was like a reflecting wall, sending back the sounds of her own hurried breathing.

She paused to rest, hoping for a lamp in a window of the Kutner place to guide her the rest of the way, but she couldn't see one.

Instead there was a light like a steady beacon much farther on, at the top of the ridge, where she was certain no one lived.

Helen walked on uneasily, losing, then picking up the light as trees intervened, and she became so fascinated with this unexpected sign of life that she almost passed by the darkened Kutner house without seeing it.

For half a minute Helen lingered in front of the house, indecisive and perplexed. Her eyes had become accustomed to the dark and from where she was she could tell that the windows were either shuttered or boarded, which meant that the Kutners had not been there for weeks, and would not return until the following May. Breaking in would be difficult and ultimately expensive—and the beacon on the crest of the ridge held her eye. Was she lost after all, or had someone built up there since the last time she had passed this way?

Helen doubted it, because Craig owned most of the land on top of the ridge, something like one hundred acres, and she felt certain that he would never give his permission for someone to move onto his property.

Without having to think about it, Helen started walking again toward the light. The road was worse, loose gravel and clay, and she slipped twice, the second time going down on one knee. Because she was wearing slacks she wasn't hurt, but as she was getting up she saw him, standing perhaps a hundred feet away in the misty wood lot.

The image of a boy in the wood lot was so compelling—like the inexplicable light above—that at first she felt only a minor current of fear. She strained to distinguish the motionless figure, but the moon was wrapped in a cloud and the figure disappeared gradually, black into black. Her eyes smarted and Helen rubbed at them, and then the fear cut into her strongly, numbing her throat, and she hurried on, not really seeing the road, heedless of falling. Even the light atop the ridge had temporarily vanished, leaving her disoriented and alone. She sobbed for breath, stopped with a jerk, looked back.

Moonlight again spread through the wood lot, but no one was there.

I saw him, she thought. I saw—

She would not let herself think of whom she had seen.

It was too late to turn around and go back. Already she had come three-quarters of the way and the ridge had leveled. The friendly light was shining, bigger than the moon, white and strong, through a gap in the woods. She would find someone there, Helen thought. Someone real who would help her.

Hawthorn, sumac and dogwood choked off the road. Helen slipped through the sharp wet leaves with an animal's desperation, soaking herself, losing her scarf. She stumbled over a root, groaned, beat branches away from her face and came into the stony clearing, where the light glittered like a huge jewel in one blackened window of the cottage in which Michael Young had lived. The light drew her closer. She touched a scratched cheek with her fingertips and went dumbly.

When she was within a few feet of the cottage, directly in front of the dazzling jagged window, she stopped, pinned down by fear. The light now seemed unearthly to her. There was nothing inside, there was no one; how had the light gotten there?

The cracked glass of the window seemed to leap out at her, a thousand dazzling pieces, and the light was gone. In the space of the window a face appeared.

Helen turned away, screaming, and caught a

glimpse of him scrambling over the windowsill, coming after her. She tried to run and fell to her knees.

A hand seized her shoulder.

"Good God," Craig Young said. "Helen? What are you doing up here?"

She recoiled from the flashlight beam against her eyes. "Craig?"

"Let me help you up. You scared the wits out of me, Helen."

"I . . . I scared *you*!"

"Are you hurt?"

"No . . . fine. I'm . . . my wagon stalled . . . on the road down there, and . . . I walked up to see if one of the summer houses was . . . occupied. Saw there was a light up here. I didn't want to come but—" She broke off and stared up at her nephew. "Craig? Have you . . . been here long?"

"I'd say about twenty minutes. One of Hap's deputies told me a gang of kids had been up this way, making themselves at home. I wanted to put a stop to it."

"Kids?" Helen repeated. "Craig, I saw a . . . I think it was a young boy . . . in the wood lot down there. Just standing between a couple of trees, watching the road. He couldn't have been more than . . . than ten, and he was alone."

"Are you sure you saw someone?"

"Craig, it wasn't a tree stump, or anything like that. I'm telling you it was a boy. Please don't let go of me. I've never felt like this, I don't think my knees will support me. It was just past the Kutner place. He was close to me, Craig."

"I'd like to find him. He may be one of the gang who's moved in here."

"Moved in?"

"I'll show you what I mean," Craig said grimly, and led her around the cottage to a space where the back door had been. Helen held back involuntarily but Craig angled the powerful beam of his flashlight inside. "Over here."

Helen stared at an Army-style bed with a mattress against one burned and blistered wall of what had been the kitchen of the house. This area was still roofed over and relatively well protected from snow and rain.

"No telling how long that's been up here," Craig said. "But the metal is rusting and the mattress has mildewed. I suppose that's no difference to the little bastards. They just throw a blanket over the mattress and make out all right."

"Craig, the boy I saw . . . he wasn't old enough for . . ." Helen paused, looking thoughtfully at the bed. "Craig, why did you smash that window? Didn't you see me?"

Craig grinned. "I saw somebody coming, and I was in the mood to give them a fright. I'm sorry; no way I could know—"

"Of course not."

"I'm going to throw that bed down the steep side of the ridge," Craig vowed, pointing his light into the depths of the gutted house, "and then one of these days when I've got a little money I'll restore this place. It'll be just the way it was."

Helen said without thinking, "I doubt if Amy—" And then she decided this was presumptuous. "I had to leave Peg in the wagon," she explained, "and I'm afraid she's going to wake up and find me gone. I didn't see your car—"

"Oh, I hid it the other side of the clearing. Are you feeling better now?"

"Much better."

"What did you say was the matter with your wagon?"

"Drowned out, I'm afraid. There was an overflow from the river and I didn't see the water in time."

"We'll get it started. If not, you can drive the Chevelle in and send somebody back for me." He shifted the light and they started back to the clearing, picking their way through heaps of stones and across a rotting timber, walking beneath the crippled oak that stood ineffectual guard over the remains of the house that only Craig seemed to care about anymore.

Peggy sat up straight in the front seat of the ranch wagon, aware that they had stopped, aware that it was dark and quiet. Somehow she knew, though she was not fully awake, they had not stopped in front of their house.

She heard someone trying to open the door behind her, and she turned her head, saying, "Mother?"

Craig braked his Chevelle halfway down the ridge and Helen pointed out the place where—as well as she could remember—she had seen the figure in the woods. Craig flashed his light among the trees, but the light revealed nothing.

"Whoever he is," Helen said, "I hope he has a home to go to. He seemed so lonely standing there, as if . . . he'd been waiting forever."

Craig said sourly, "I thought you didn't get a good look."

"It wasn't what I saw, it was what I felt— Craig!"

They both heard Peggy's voice at the same time,

a faint echo to it, as if she were crying from the depths of a well.

"Mother! Mother . . ."

Craig put the car in gear and gunned down the hill, headlights illuminating the tall trees on both sides of the road, pooling suddenly on the blacktop road below.

"There she is!" Helen said. "Stop, Craig, let me out!"

Peggy scrambled toward them, and Helen threw open the door and ran to meet her.

"I saw him, Mother! Michael was here! He came right up to the car!"

Helen hugged her daughter tightly, but Peggy tried to pull away.

"Let's find him, Mother! He was right here!"

"Baby . . ."

Craig came loping toward them. "What's the matter, was she having a nightmare?"

"Uncle Craig, I saw Michael! He looked in the window at me, and then he disappeared!"

"He ran away?" said Craig, looking stunned.

"No, he disappeared! Like a ghost."

"Peggy . . . Peg," Helen said urgently. "Calm down now. Tell me exactly what happened."

Peggy was not about to calm down, but she said more precisely, "I woke up and you weren't there, and then I heard him trying to open the door and I turned around and it was Michael. When I looked at him he disappeared. So I got out of the car, but by then he was gone."

Craig trotted over to the ranch wagon with his flashlight in his hand, studied the gravel below the right-side door, then went on more deliberately along the shoulder of the blacktop, aiming his flashlight here and there. Helen lifted Peggy and carried her toward the wagon.

"He was here, Mother!" the wide-eyed Peggy insisted.

"Yes, yes, I believe you. But he's gone now. Peggy, he's gone and he's not coming back. So we might as well go home, don't you think?"

"Can we come back in the morning? I want to see him."

Helen felt as if she were going to cry. "I don't know ... maybe he doesn't want us to see him. We'll t-talk about it in the morning."

"Are you all right, Mother? Where was Uncle Craig?"

"The car stalled. I went to find help and fortunately for us he came along."

"I told Michael to wait. I told him I wasn't going to hurt him. I told him! Why did he disappear?"

Craig had come back; Helen glanced at him hopefully but he just shrugged and looked doubtfully at Peggy.

"No footprints ... except a couple that must be yours, Helen."

"Uncle Craig, what's the matter with Michael? Is he mad at us?"

Craig ignored the question. "Could I have your keys, Helen? I'll see if I can get this thing started."

He unlocked the driver's door and slid in under the wheel of the ranch wagon. Nothing happened when he turned the key in the ignition. Then he got out, lifted the hood, studied the alternator for a few seconds, made an adjustment, slammed the hood, reached inside the wagon and switched on the lights, which then worked perfectly.

"Did I do something wrong?" Helen asked timidly.

"Just a loose connection," Craig muttered. "Take it easy driving home and you'll get there all right. Better have all the wiring checked first thing in the morning."

"In the car, baby," Helen said, depositing Peggy on the front seat. Peg scrambled to the far window and stared intently out at the dark. She seemed disappointed when Michael didn't appear, somewhat like a firefly, to justify her close attention.

"Better speak to her," Craig said in a low voice. "Or everyone in The Shades is going to get the impression that we have a family ghost on our hands."

"Don't we?" Helen replied.

Craig hung his head, looking tired and disgusted.

"If there's another explanation, I hope we won't be long in hearing it. But until then, I *saw* him tonight, and Peggy saw ... Michael, and we weren't having the same nightmare. He did just disappear both times like a—like an apparition. Can you tell me what a little boy would be doing way out in the woods this time of the night, Craig?"

Craig started to speak, shook his head in resignation, then said, "I'll let *him* tell me. He's hiding, whoever he is. Maybe I can flush him out of the woods—"

Helen put a hand on his arm. "Don't stay around, Craig," she pleaded. "Please don't! Go home, or go to Amy's, but get away from here."

"Helen, you're—"

"I'm scared silly," Helen finished for him, and she didn't care at all that Peggy was listening.

8

The last busload of boys from the Greenleaf School left the campus at five-fifteen on the Saturday afternoon of the Old Settlers' Reunion, and Amy gratefully returned to her office to change into more casual clothes and lock up for the weekend.

Once she had dressed in hip huggers, a cashmere sweater and a red babushka, she took a small gift-wrapped package from a desk drawer, walked down the first-floor corridor of the school's administration building and knocked lightly at Craig's door. When he didn't respond right away, Amy opened the door herself and looked in.

He was asprawl in a leather armchair in one corner of the office, reading glasses halfway down his nose, and he was making rapid notes on a pad of paper. The only light in the office came from the Tensor lamp on a shelf above his head: he had drawn the blinds of the windows that overlooked the quadrangle of the Greenleaf School.

"You're on overtime," Amy admonished, and Craig looked up quickly.

"Oh, Amy. What time is it getting to be?" He took off the black-rimmed glasses and set them on the pad in his lap.

"Time for us to go, or we'll miss the fun."

"Some fun," Craig said with a yawn. "The eighteenth annual Old Settlers' Reunion. So far it's been exactly like the previous seventeen. Always rains, and we end up jammed indoors at the school auditorium, damp and uncomfortable, telling each other what a great reunion we'll have next year."

Amy crossed the office and opened the blinds, letting in the rays of the setting sun. "Nothing but broken clouds," she said triumphantly. "The gods of the reunion have been kind." When Craig didn't respond or move from his chair, Amy looked at him with a hint of suspicion and said, "You're not exactly ecstatic. I have a hunch I'm going to be enjoying the sights by myself tonight."

"Uh . . . if you wouldn't mind, Amy, I'd like to get these session notes in order while I'm in a working mood. Probably won't take me but another hour."

"We're supposed to meet Helen at five-thirty, remember?"

Craig blinked. "Now I do. I promise, I'll catch up to you on the midway." He noticed the birthday-wrapped package in her hand and said, "For Peg? What's the occasion?"

"No, it's something I picked up for Peter, one of those tricky interlocking wooden puzzles. I gave

106

up trying to solve it after three days. Peter will solve it before bedtime, I'm sure."

"I thought he was getting out of the infirmary this afternoon."

"Mrs. Cagle says he's still running a temperature, and the doctor won't OK his release. I feel so sorry for him, he'll miss the fun, and he desperately needs a little fun in his life." Amy opened her purse and took out a card. "Will you sign this? The gift will mean a whole lot more if it's from both of us."

"Sure." Craig put his signature on the card, then grinned sorrowfully. "This might mean he won't bother to open the present. Pete and I haven't been on the best of terms the past couple of weeks. In fact he's been pretty damned hostile. On the other hand, I've been too demanding, I think. But I expect a little more communication from a boy with his intelligence."

"You'll get it," Amy said. "Don't be discouraged."

"After almost a year I'm not even sure we're friends." Craig stared at the golden windows.

"If Dr. Tomlinson is satisfied with the progress you've made, then I think you should be. And I think you ought to put those notes away and come along. You could use a little fun yourself."

"I promise, Amy—another hour at the most."

Amy stood over Craig for a few moments; he looked sheepish and conciliatory so she bent to kiss him.

"I'm on my way," she said briskly. "But if I miss the fireworks on your account I'm going to be as uncommunicative as Peter Mathis for the next couple of weeks, bank on that."

After leaving Craig, Amy hurried upstairs to the

second-floor infirmary, where Mrs. Cagle, the nurse on duty, greeted her.

"Is Peter asleep? I wanted to leave this with him; it's sort of a get-well-quick present."

"No, no, come in, Amy." They went through a screened doorway into the shadowy ward, which Peter Mathis had to himself that afternoon. He was sitting propped up in bed with a thermometer in his mouth, a small-boned nine-year-old with large brown eyes and an overgrowth of dark brown hair. He had flawless skin which was unusually white except for smudges under the eyes. Those eyes could hurt you, Amy had discovered upon first meeting Peter Mathis. Of all the boys at the school he was her favorite, but he was also the hardest to befriend, as Craig had observed.

"I hear you're feeling better," Amy said. Peter's expression didn't change. He watched Amy as narrowly as he had watched when she entered the ward. He undoubtedly had seen the gift in her hand, but it was not his style to demonstrate interest.

Amy put the little package on the bed near his hand. "Craig picked this out," she lied. "He thought you'd enjoy working with it if you got tired of reading."

Peter stared at her with an intensity that some people took for rudeness, but Amy was used to that; she returned an unperturbed smile. "It might not be any fun," she suggested. "It's a puzzle, and it's awfully difficult; I couldn't work it myself."

She had said enough to interest him; his eyes flickered, taking in the beribboned package. Then Peter blinked, deliberately, thanking her.

"Your dinner's here," Mrs. Cagle said, as the

buzzer sounded outside, and she went to receive the tray from the cafeteria.

"It's okra and swiss steak," Amy said sympathetically, wrinkling her nose. "I'll come by tomorrow and bring you something good from the midway. Do you like fried pies? So do I, and the Eastern Star ladies are selling the best fried pies I ever ate." Amy pointed to the present. "Let me know how you make out with that," she said jauntily. "I'll have to run now." She was not in quite the hurry that she pretended, she would have liked to spend a few more minutes with Peter, but his physical isolation in the lonely infirmary grieved her, and she knew of no way to cheer him up.

Outside it was windy but not particularly cold, and the sky was rapidly clearing; already the stars had begun to come out in the dimming blue. Amy walked with her hands in the pockets of her parka, depressed because she had literally run out on Peter Mathis, depressed because Craig was not with her. When she reached the drive where she'd left the black Mustang, she turned for a lingering look at his office windows, saw nothing, not even the reading light, and with a sigh got into her car.

It had been a bad week for Craig, with all the talk of a ghost, of a "haunt" in the valley of The Shades. The story of the Youngs had been revived and was one of the favored topics of conversation, supplanting even a recent and spectacular bus-truck collision on U.S. 43. A couple of earnest citizens had reported seeing the ghost of Michael Young to the sheriff, who had reluctantly but painstakingly checked the stories, finding them to be cases of mistaken identity. And Craig had received a couple of telephone calls from a youth who thought he was being enormously funny.

Despite the foolishness, Amy thought, there were a good many people who took the ghost story, with all its ramifications, seriously. She was no longer sure that she was among them, because Craig's cumulative reaction to the episodes disturbed her, forced her to side with him. He had nearly come to blows with a well-meaning farmer after the official opening of the reunion the night before, because the man had offered the services of a relative who was "in touch" with the other side, and willing to try to contact the spirit of Michael Young.

Amy shuddered as she drove through a swirl of red leaves to the gates of the school, but she managed a smile for Mr. Allison, one of the night watchmen, who was on duty there. She couldn't blame Craig for wanting to avoid the reunion, and the inevitable stares; she had the melancholy feeling that his "hour of work" would stretch into several hours, and that he would show up only after the crowds had thinned, with an abject apology, eager to take her someplace where they could be alone, where he could be at peace for a while.

"Yes," she said, half aloud, and smiled again, feeling her cheeks growing hot. But she felt much better all of a sudden.

Despite the excitement over Michael Young, at least a week had passed with no further word from the boy who had started the whole thing—from "Michael" himself. He had not been seen, or heard from. Amy was thankful for that, and she thought seriously, looking at the milky porcelain sky, *Maybe it's all over now. . . .*

Maybe the spirit of Michael Young had been among them, and moved on, having satisfied his purpose. Could he have found what Craig needed so badly, peace of mind?

Amy felt sorry that she would never know for sure.

The main street of the village of The Shades had been closed and transformed into a three-block-long midway, at the east end of which the two dozen clanking rides and assorted thrill attractions of the Brinkley Brothers Carnival were twined in popping eye-watering blister-bright neon. Because the reunion was the traditional climax to the fall tourist season and because the night had turned fair and mild, both the midway and the carnival grounds were packed. Hap Washbrook had all his boys in harness and the Highway Patrol had sent over a couple of cars to keep traffic moving through the various detours, but Hap himself was not working too hard.

Earlier in the evening he had joined the foursome of Helen, Amy, Peg and Doremus, treated them to dinner at the fried-chicken booth run by the Women's Auxiliary of the VFW, then escorted them to the rides. There the two men left Amy and Helen behind and took the delighted Peggy for a whirl on the carousel.

"What are you in the mood for now, Peggy?" Hap asked, helping her down at the end of the ride; Peg looked around deliberately and then pointed at the rickety-looking Ferris Wheel. Helen blanched, but Doremus took her hand and off they went.

The two pounds of steel badge on Hap's shirt got them preferential treatment at the Ferris wheel. Doremus and Peggy took the first available seat and were swung aloft.

"Oh, Lord," Helen muttered.

"Looks like a piece of junk," Hap conceded, "but I checked it out myself bolt for bolt. Amy, let's you and me grab the next seat."

One of his deputies, a tall youth with a slouch and a massive pearl-handled pistol on his hip, came up behind Hap and said in his ear, "Sheriff, Enoch says can you come down to the jail for a few minutes."

Hap scowled. "What for?"

"You got a phone call."

"Good Christ," Hap said. "I'm busy. Take a message."

"Enoch done that already."

Hap gave the deputy a suffering look and said patiently, "What was it?"

"He didn't tell me. Said to find you and ask can you come down to the jail. . . ."

Hap looked with genuine longing at the Ferris wheel, and then glanced regretfully at Amy. He said, loud enough to be heard over the cacophony of shrieks and wheeler-dealer carnival music, "Something I have to attend to, girls. I'll find you all in about ten minutes or so," and went striding off, with the deputy at his side.

Twenty-five minutes later he hadn't returned.

"No telling what's keeping him," Doremus said, when they got together following Peggy's third ride on the carousel. "But it could be something that'll have Hap tied up the rest of the evening."

Peg was flushed and big-eyed from excitement. "Could I ride on the Ferris wheel again, Mother?"

"It's a quarter to eight now and you have to be at the park, in costume, by eight-twenty; I think we'd better go."

"Oh, one more *time*," Peggy said, hanging like a rag doll from her mother's hand.

"Straighten up and act your age, please. Amy, do you want to stay in case Craig—"

"I'd never find him if he did show up; there's just too much of a crowd." She smiled at Doremus, a smile of apology which he failed to understand. "If you don't mind, I'll ride along with the three of you. I wouldn't want to miss Peggy's dramatic debut."

Peggy, happy to oblige, struck a pose and chanted, " 'Indians surrounded the little log cabin, but Mary Gatewood was not afraid.' "

"I seem to have heard that somewhere before," Helen remarked, with an expression that brought a rare grin to Doremus' normally impassive face. "Well, here's hoping Hap doesn't feel we ran out on him."

"Sooner or later Hap'll be at the park," Amy said. "We'll see him again."

He had been sitting in the unmarked patrol car for over an hour now, with the lights turned off and the radio turned off, and his eyes were stinging from the effort of focusing through powerful binoculars in an attempt to distinguish movement on either side of the brimming and turbulent Competition River, which gave the state park its name.

He was parked about a hundred yards from the designated meeting place and he had managed to drive into the park quietly, showing no lights, and find a well-concealed observation point, maneuvering his car by memory and the moon. He had felt confident that this was a good ploy and that sooner or later the one he had come to meet would become rattled or discouraged and give himself away. But just the opposite had occurred: Hap found himself restless and bored, and the feeling was growing on him that he'd been had.

His back ached and he craved a cigarette. There had been no sign of anyone at the shuttered trail house or on the high footbridge that crossed the free-flowing river and the leaning balks of stone which defined the river's course. As far as he knew he was utterly alone, while not so far away and below him, two or three thousand people had gathered on the picnic green in front of the river falls to witness the reunion pageant—or rather tolerate the pageant, which depicted the history of Shades County. There would be fireworks later, and Hap hated the idea of missing the fireworks, especially since he'd already wasted a good part of the evening. . . . He raised the binoculars again for a quick look near the footbridge and this time saw something among the piled stones, a pulse of white like moonlight quick on a dull mirror: something pale and nebulous, a face perhaps. But it was only a flash and there was no repetition.

Hap Washbrook let out a sigh and cursed himself for gullibility in the line of duty. Take a look, he thought: have it over with. Nothing to be afraid of.

He was so certain now that he'd been tricked by that phone call that he could admit he'd been uneasy in the beginning. So he had come creeping up the summit road and stopped a good distance away from the stony-sided rush of river and waited, waited to be sure in his bones that he had not been talking to a ghost.

The garbled amplified voices from below had ceased, and Hap looked at the luminous face of his chronometer, which gave the time as ten minutes to nine.

Be starting the fireworks soon.

Hap grunted and reached for the big six-battery electric torch clipped to the underside of the dashboard; his eyes shifted to the pump-action shotgun that always rode with him in the front seat.

"What for?" he asked himself, after serious thought about the need for such a weapon, but he was uneasy again and so he sprung the fully loaded shotgun from the clamp that held it upright and got out of the car, closing the door noiselessly behind him.

He walked along with surprising quickness for a large man, the electric torch swinging in his right hand, shotgun level in the left hand. He had no need of the light yet, no need to announce himself.

There was a satisfying crumpling sound overhead, and a violet smoky bloom. Hap turned his head for a look.

Get their money's worth this year, he thought. *Two thousand bucks just for fireworks.*

Whoosh!

Goddam beautiful, Hap thought, walking backward. *Really lights up the sky. Really lights up old Hap.* He glanced at the torch in his hand. *What the hell, might as well use this thing.*

There was a twenty-second silence following the green-and-yellow burst against the black sky, and then half a dozen sharp cracks—those were the little spiraling ones; he didn't know what they were called.

Hap reached the edge of the river, thinking about Amy. God, how she could give a man agony just standing next to him! Terrible waste of a good woman if she married that nephew of Helen's. He looked broodingly across the water, raised his light, played it on the jumble of stones thrown down from the break in the ridge perhaps centuries ago. The sound of the water was quite loud. There was a searing whiteness behind him, then a scarlet glow.

He followed the river to the trail house, where the footbridge arched, trying to hear something besides the bubbling of the river. The house was securely padlocked as it should have been, tightly shuttered for the night. There were no surprises waiting.

I suppose I'll have to cross the bridge, he thought.

The sky crackled.

See it pretty good from up here.

Midway on the bridge he stopped and beamed his light down into the broken quarry of limestone, slab on slab, wet from the slashing river.

He glimpsed the thrown rock a second before it hit him, and he flinched just enough, getting his left arm up, to deflect it away from his face. It was a small rock but it stung his forearm, and he forgot all about the array of fireworks in the night sky.

Hurried probing with his light showed him nothing, and he never saw the second whizzing stone at all. It flicked off the bridge rail and shot away into darkness.

Hap figured he'd better get the hell off the bridge.

Crouching, he followed the beam of his torch to the far side and half slid down a slope of stone into a narrow space where the waters of the river lapped coldly at the soles of his boots.

A rocket boomed emphatically overhead, loosing a shower of crimson embers, and the stones that wedged the sheriff to the river glowed for a moment.

"All right, I'm here!" Hap shouted angrily. "Where are you?"

He thought he heard something downstream— a rock dislodged into water. He stepped out ankle deep into the tugging river and shot his light along the edge. The beam carried a good quarter of a mile, fading at last into the woods where the river began its fall.

Hap plunged recklessly through the water, searching with his light, and he was rewarded by the sight of a leaping shadow. He climbed ashore, sorry now that he had brought the shotgun, which was only in his way. He skinned his knuckles, cursed under his breath and shimmied over a moss-covered boulder. He dropped, gasping, on the other side, his light sweeping across a broad tongue of gravel to the tree-studded wall of ridge looming above him.

"I've got a loaded shotgun here," Hap yelled. "And I'm using it."

His hearing was affected by the constant low roar of the river, but all the same he could not mistake the sound which seemed to come out of the darkness only a few inches behind his head, a terrible, animal sighing that shocked his heart still.

Something like a baseball bat swung with maniacal force hit him on the left arm just above the elbow, snapping the bone. Hap screamed and the shotgun clattered to the rocks at his feet. The force of the blow knocked Hap to one side and his feet slipped on the slightly pitched, slick-surfaced rock he'd been standing on. He fell, cracking the lens of his flashlight, and plummeted up to his chest in the numbing river.

The cold water helped him to recover from the first sickening burst of pain and he struggled to keep from being pulled along by the current. Somehow, without losing his grip on the flashlight, he managed to inch his way back up the slanted stone, to drag himself free of the river. With his right arm extended, Hap lifted the beam of the flashlight and saw, through a haze of pain, who had assaulted him. He was almost as shocked as he had been to hear Michael's voice over the telephone. For a few seconds he wasn't even aware of the fact that the shotgun he had dropped was now pointed at him.

"You loved my mother, didn't you? You sneaked around and you made love to her, but you wouldn't stand up for her!"

Hap scarcely heard him. He concentrated on not slipping into the river again, on finding a niche for his feet, on easing carefully to his knees. The pain in his broken arm was excruciating but he'd been in pain many times, he knew how to ignore it and set to work.

The sky was lighted once more, in tones of gold and strawberry pink, but there was a deadly roaring in his ears which cut out all sound. Hap had no definite plans, except to stand on his feet again. Nothing else seemed so important to him, not even the fact that he was in the company of an Imp of Death. But he had another look at the shotgun as he dragged himself up; to his horror there was a pinching in his stomach, a bitterness of dread.

"That tears a man up," he heard himself say. "Please God, don't shoot me with it." And he heard a skyrocket going up. The sky dissolved in streamers of green. There were earnest words in Hap's mind, on the tip of his tongue. It was an incredible feeling, being there with an Imp of Death, under the muzzle of his own gun, pinned by those long-dead and hating eyes: *it would never happen and morning would come along*. He would get out of bed at the usual time and put on the starched forest-green shirt with the big weight of polished badge and go down the street to Madge's place for his eye-opening cup of coffee, and it would be *Hello, Sheriff*, as usual. Another rocket whistled dismally. *See it good from up here*, Hap thought. He said hopelessly, humbly, choking on his words, "That thing tears a man up," and in the next instant his chest was ripped open by the double-aught shot, he followed his own sprayed blood out into the river, and disappeared.

The screeches and throaty whisperings and scintillating whistles and vibrant poppings and ear-pounding booms had reached a crescendo and the sky was almost continually ablaze now, saturated and molten. From her perch astride Doremus' neck Peggy watched with a sleepy satiated eye, and yawned.

With a final volley the sky went to black again, and the crowd on the picnic grounds that fronted the hundred-foot Competition Falls began to stir and think of the traffic jam that was to follow.

"Is that all?" Peggy said in an aggrieved voice, and Amy reached over to pat her knee. Peggy was still wearing the version of a pioneer dress that Helen had painstakingly sewn for her for the pageant, and her cheeks were deeply red from rouge. She had said her one line with clarity and such

119

gusto that she had received a round of startled applause from adults wearied by dozens of mumbling children.

"I don't think that was the grand finale," Helen said, wishing they weren't so close to the falls. It was a long way to the parking lot, and she had been on her feet for several hours. She wondered if Doremus would mind if she just leaned on him for a few minutes, and then she wondered if she wasn't a little giddy from fatigue.

"What's a grand finale?" Peggy asked.

Helen started to explain but the grand finale was under way, rockets' red glare and patriotic streamers of blue and white unfurling above the glowing falls.

Ahhhh, they all said, gratefully, and began to think of home, began to turn away.

And then the thing came down the falls, in a torrent of white water, came fast, slowed, turned, slipped past jutting ice-slick rocks, turned a little more, head lolling, arms flopping, was washed downward to a level a dozen feet above the deep foaming pool at the base of the falls.

Ahhhh! they said, amazed, and they lingered to puzzle over this thing that seemed a joke, that could not be accepted for what it was obviously meant to be, a dead body, because the Old Settlers' Reunion had come to its customary reassuring end, and they were ready to go.

The thing in the falls hung motionless for several seconds on the ledge where it had dropped, and then the jetting pressure of water behind it pushed it gently forward, and for an instant before it plunged down into the floodlit pool it emerged from the curtain of white water in its shredded green shirt and the big handsome shotgunned badge on the shirt glittered. The vacant eyes of Hap Washbrook surveyed them all pensively.

"Oh, my God!" Helen said, and hid her face from the sight of Hap's cut-string sprawl into the deep river pool.

9

The highway patrol car stopped in front of the Connellys' at ten minutes after one in the morning, and Doremus got out. Helen was on the lookout for him, and she took him back to the kitchen, where Craig and Amy waited. They all appeared red-eyed and dreary from fatigue. They were drinking whiskey; Doremus looked at the decanter on the table with undisguised longing. Helen poured a couple of ounces of the whiskey for him while Craig and Amy sprang questions.

Doremus was exhausted himself from climbing over the boulders of the Competition River, and his hands shook as he grasped the shot glass. He deferred answers to their questions until he had sipped about an ounce of the whiskey and lighted a cigar.

"Hap's car was parked not too far from the footbridge and the trail house above the falls," he said then. "Partly concealed, as if he'd been staked out. Finding where he went into the river was easy; he'd dropped his flashlight and we homed in on the beam. His shotgun was right there too, fired once. From the condition of Hap's body when he was pulled out, he'd been shot at close range."

"By whom?" Craig demanded.

Doremus tackled his whiskey again. "By himself," he muttered.

Amy's expression was incredulous; she shook her head in protest. Doremus glanced at her and then explained. "From appearances, Hap was there looking for something, or somebody. He lost his footing and dropped the gun. It went off either when he dropped it or when he tried to pick it up. That's the best explanation anyone has right now. In the morning the Patrol will go over that area inch by inch, and by tomorrow night there may be some conclusions from the autopsy which will change the story."

Craig said, "You don't think it was an accident."

"Hap had handled guns all his life. It's unlikely he would have dropped one. Unlikely, but not impossible."

"What if there was a fight, and somebody took his shotgun away?" Amy suggested. "You said he was up there on a—a stakeout. That means he was expecting someone, doesn't it?" Amy's expression changed, and she became so excited she almost upset the untouched glass of whiskey in front of her. "Helen, remember when the deputy came looking for Hap earlier tonight? I didn't hear much of the conversation, but the deputy said Hap had had a telephone call, and it was important for him to go down to the courthouse! That call must have had something to do with Hap's murder."

"It isn't exactly murder," Doremus reminded her. He gave the decanter a friendly look and Helen poured for him again, saying:

"What matters is that Hap is dead. And The Shades doesn't seem like such a pleasant place to live anymore." She sat back tensely, hands in her lap.

Craig glanced at Amy, who nodded, and they got up together. "It's late," Craig said, "and we ought to be going. Helen, why don't we all get together at my place tomorrow afternoon?" He glanced at Doremus, hesitated, then said, "You too, Doremus."

"Thanks," Doremus said, smiling, but he seemed intent on other things.

"Do you have a way home?" Amy asked him.

"Oh, sure."

Helen said, "Craig, I don't know about tomorrow. I'll call."

"All right, Helen. No, don't get up."

Once they were on the walk outside, Amy said, in a misguided effort to cheer Craig. "They're becoming very much aware of each other, have you noticed?"

"What?"

"You didn't notice. It's the way Doremus looks at Helen. I don't think he's recognized that he's falling, but I'm sure—"

Craig scowled. "Amy, for God's sake."

Amy was silent until they drove away from the house in Craig's car, and then she said defensively, "It's time for Helen to marry again. She needs marriage." A glint appeared in Amy's eye. "Most people do."

Craig shifted gears roughly. "If she decided to marry it wouldn't be to that . . . tramp fisherman, or whatever he is."

"That isn't fair to Doremus. He's hard to get to know, but—And I don't think he'll spend the rest of his life lying around a riverbank; he isn't suited for that. For one thing, he's not so much older than Helen—I'd say he's about forty-five. He has sort of a neglected look; it ages him. I think Doremus is recovering from something; he's finding himself." Craig's eyes were narrowed, as if he were in pain. "I hope Helen will give him a chance. After all, how many eligible men will she meet in this—"

"Amy, would you please quit speculating. Look, I've got a damned awful headache, and I—"

" 'Keep your distance, Amy.' I only waited four hours for you tonight."

Criag stopped suddenly in the middle of the empty street and glanced at Amy. She was hurt, and not hiding it particularly well.

"I'm sorry," he said, after a difficult half minute of silence.

"That's familiar."

"No, really, Amy, I—" His face crumpled and Amy had the alarming notion that he was about to cry. She'd never seen him in tears. But he suppressed his emotion grimly and said in a low voice, "I don't feel well, but I . . . want you with me tonight. All night, Amy. I've never needed you more than I do now." He pressed his forehead against the steering wheel, eyes closed. He was rigid until Amy touched his shoulder, exploring his mood.

"What's wrong, Craig?"

"Helen said it. The Shades isn't such a pleasant place to live anymore. I've spent my life here, and now something evil has moved in, and I'm afraid, I'm actually afraid. Of *him*, Amy. Of Michael, my brother."

She was stunned.

"I believe it now. I believe it's Michael. Somehow he killed them both, Amy."

"Michael didn't have anything to do with Hap's death. He . . . he wasn't there."

"Wasn't he?" Craig said, with another, horrified look at her. "How do we know?"

Doremus finished his third glass of whiskey, feeling pleasantly flushed in the warm kitchen. Helen sat as quietly as she had been sitting all evening. She had discovered it was useless trying to keep her thoughts away from the sight of Hap, so torn and pathetically loose-jointed, spilling madly down the sparkling falls. It was easier for her to breathe when she went over the tragedy many times. Repetition dulled the shock; the prospect of healing tears seemed less remote.

She said politely, "Would you like another drink, Doremus?" She only wished that he would go, even though she dreaded being alone. But she was afraid of some greater horror, as yet undiscovered; there was a suggestion of this horror in the detective's pensive eyes.

"No, thank you," Doremus replied. "Much more whiskey and I'll turn into a roaring drunk. A roaring boring drunk."

Helen smiled tentatively. "I can't imagine you roaring."

Doremus leaned forward, hands clenched on the table. "I got that way once a year," he said. "Had to do it, to take the pressure off." He nodded emphatically. "You can't imagine the work that goes into solving a murder case: plain hard work. Oh, once every two or three years we were lucky, we broke a case in a hurry. But—"

There was an empty water glass in front of Helen; Doremus reached for it abruptly and poured a slug of whiskey for her. Helen looked puzzled.

"Would you drink that?" he asked. "You're not looking too well. Those circles under your eyes . . . My wife had liver trouble, and she got terrible circles. . . . Go ahead, drink up."

Helen didn't care for whiskey and she was about to tell him so, but he looked at her so earnestly, with a high flush in his cheeks, that she couldn't refuse him. She nipped at the whiskey. "I don't feel bad," she explained. "I'm . . . I'm just over-tired."

"You have the horrors, and I don't blame you." He winked at her, solemnly. Helen felt so startled by the incongruity that she drank a good deal more of her whiskey and presently, after it stopped burning in her nearly empty stomach, she found it had a soothing effect. The whiskey stilled a need to shudder, it brought the kitchen walls a little closer and mellowed the light above the table. She looked in fascination at Doremus' clenched hands. *Awfully late*, she thought, but that didn't seem to matter so much. His hands looked rough and strong and it comforted her to study them.

He filled her glass again, hesitated, then filled his own. When he sat back the chair creaked under his weight. The clock above the stove whirred in the silence. Helen, feeling bold, feeling ready, drank.

"Michael called Hap tonight, didn't he?" she

asked Doremus, and the detective, after a moment's hesitation, nodded.

Helen felt a dolorous urge to laugh. "And then he killed Hap."

"I don't know what went on up there. Michael is just a voice on the telephone to me, so far."

. "What did he say to Hap?"

"Only Hap knew. The deputy who took the call—Enoch, Enoch Mills; know him?—didn't have too much to tell."

"But it *was* Michael. Just a voice on the telephone, you say, but he can be anywhere, he can see anything, he wants to kill us!"

Doremus looked up sharply. "Why did you say that?"

Helen seemed shaken and lost.

"Has he threatened you? Was there a call you haven't told me about?"

"No . . ."

"Then why did you say he wants to kill you?"

"Because he must hate me! Because he . . . came back, and his mother wasn't there, she was dead . . . she died, she died in that place where I had her put away, and he blames me, he blames me, he always did and he—" Helen cut herself off with an anxious jerk of her head and stared helplessly at Doremus. "I have to stop thinking like that," she said softly.

"Those two boys were running wild," Doremus said, "and your sister had no control over them—no control over herself, according to Hap." Helen grimaced at his choice of words but Doremus went on. "And I don't see where you had a choice in committing her to a sanitarium. She died, which was unfortunate, but you had to try to help her."

"I wish now I'd never come to The Shades."

Helen got up and walked to the back door, looked out through the glass. "No, I don't think I mean that; I loved Ed, and where would I be without Peggy? But I doubt if I have the ... the courage to live through it all again. Poor scared Alice and Michael, Michael, always running away, I couldn't help him at all." She bowed her head. "I've had to resist running away myself, taking Peggy out of school and going ... somewhere. But I won't have Peggy living afraid and besides, I'm not sure it would do any good. Wouldn't answer the telephone or open the door no matter where I was. Because ... it might be Michael. That lost little boy. Two days ago when I was waiting at school for Peg one of the Waldrup boys came up behind me. He doesn't even look that much like Michael, but for a few seconds I was so shocked I thought I was going to faint. In broad daylight. I've told myself too many times that it's nonsense, there are no ghosts, but then I think, 'What if?' Two of my friends are dead, who knows why, and he keeps on calling, calling."

Doremus studied her glumly, but he had nothing to say that might comfort her; he was too involved with the riddle of Michael Young. Presently he asked, as if he were thinking aloud, "How did Michael get along with Dr. Britton?"

"Get along ... ? I don't think Michael saw much of him. Andy might have treated him once or twice for a cold or one of the usual childhood illnesses, but I don't remember specifically. I scarcely knew Andy myself in those days."

"Was Hap the sheriff then?"

"Yes." She didn't wait for Doremus to ask, but said immediately, "And Michael knew him a little better than he did Andy. On two occasions when

Michael ran away he was found and handed down the line by state authorities, eventually reaching Hap, who always took the time to drive him home. Hap treated Michael very well, sympathetically. I'd say Hap went out of his way to befriend Michael. But of course none of us had any luck there."

"Suppose Michael was alive today—can you think of any reason why he'd want those two men dead?"

"Alive?" Helen said, startled. "Do you think—"

"I don't know what I think," Doremus replied patiently, "I'm just taking ideas out of the air. What about it, Helen? I know the boy resented you, but what could he have held against Hap and the doctor? It could be a little thing, actually, warped out of proportion by the passing of time. People have been murdered for any number of reasons, and not always by the criminally insane. So if Michael— Wait a minute."

The detective's eyes glittered. "I could be asking the wrong questions. It's not how they treated *him* that matters; it's how they treated his mother." He looked to Helen for confirmation, but she seemed bewildered. "Is there any chance that Dr. Britton could have been making love to your sister?"

"What an ugly— Of course not!"

"As far as you know. But he was well acquainted with Alice, and admittedly she had a lot of boyfriends. He could easily have been one of them. If he was and if it went on for any length of time, then his wife probably knew about it. I'll have to ask her."

"You couldn't ask Elsa something like that!"

"Yes, I could. I'm used to being indelicate."

130

"You certainly are," Helen said furiously, but her anger turned to mortification and she stared out into the dark again. Doremus seemed not to have noticed her remark. He said:

"Hap was a born womanizer, I know that for sure, and he wouldn't have overlooked someone as attractive as your sister."

"I don't think," Helen said in a strangled voice, "that it was just a . . . casual affair, although it probably started that way, for both of them. In the end Hap acted as if he loved her, despite all the trouble she caused him. He saw as clearly as I did that she had to have psychiatric care. He rode with me the day I took Alice to the sanitarium. He kept her laughing as long as he could, kept her from thinking about being locked up."

"So you and Hap made the decision to have your sister committed. And she had to be certified incompetent by a physician."

"Andy signed the papers."

Doremus said reflectively, "A psychotic personality might find that enough justification for killing the doctor—for arranging his death. Was your sister committed by court order?"

"Yes. The judge was a man named Schofield. But he died several years ago." Doremus looked questioningly at her. "I think it was a heart attack. He was a very old man." Helen came back to the table slowly and sat down, looking more intrigued than frightened. "I don't see how Michael could have survived that snowstorm. After all, his coat was found; I identified it. Bones were found. It couldn't have been some other little boy."

"As far as I know, there wasn't a medical examination to determine how long the remains had been in the open. There was no attempt to match the teeth in the skull with dental charts. Hap did a sloppy job. It could easily have been another boy, one who had wandered off from the Greenleaf School months or possibly years before Michael Young was lost. I don't think it would be too difficult to check that out. Your nephew could do it for me."

"I can't believe Michael is alive," Helen said stubbornly. "If he is, where has he been? How has he managed to live?"

"By his wits," Doremus suggested. "He wasn't a baby when he disappeared. From all I've heard, he was a boy with a lot of determination, and he knew the woods, he knew how to protect himself." Doremus toyed with an unlighted cigar, thinking. "I'd much rather believe in a live Michael than a ghost," he said firmly. "If he's alive then probably he's been living here in The Shades, or nearby, for some time. You might have passed him down in the village a hundred times. He knows you, of course, but you'd never recognize him." Helen started to protest. "No, you wouldn't. Michael Young seems to be a clever, well-motivated and disciplined homicidal maniac. He scares me."

"What about the telephone calls, Doremus? That isn't a man calling. It's a little boy."

"That's one of the ways he scares me, with his elaborate playacting. Apparently he's worked this whole thing out carefully. It's significant that he called you first."

Helen looked at him uncomprehendingly.

"I'm sure it gave him a great deal of pleasure, settling up with the doctor and with Hap, but in a way they were incidental participants in the tragedy of his mother. You're the one who will have to suffer most for what happened to her. You came down here and meddled in their lives and sent the mother away to die. You're the one he came to hate with the kind of pathological bitterness that could eventually turn him into a murderer." Helen closed her eyes and looked momentarily ill. Doremus fidgeted unhappily and said, in an attempt to be soothing, "But he's not a ghost and, dangerous as he is, he's not omnipresent either. I think we'll—"

He was startled when Helen left the table and half ran from the kitchen, and he rose to follow her. But, as he heard her going up the stairs, he sensed what was on her mind and returned to the kitchen to polish off the whiskey in his glass. He barely tasted it. While he was cleaning up and rinsing the dishes in the sink, Helen returned, still unnaturally pale but looking relieved.

"I'm sorry. I thought that . . . I had to see if Peg—"

"How was she?"

"Sound asleep." Helen looked fearfully at him. "You said he wants me to suffer. Do you think he'll try to hurt me through Peggy? If he's insane, then, he's capable—"

"I don't know what he'll try to do next," Doremus admitted. "So far he's been bright enough or cautious enough to stay away from this house. But if I've guessed right and you are next on his list, he'll have to come now." Helen took that with no flicker of emotion, but her hands as she gripped the back of a chair were bloodless.

"How can we find him?" she asked. "Before he calls, before he comes? I don't know if I can take—"

Doremus said gently, "In the morning I'll talk to Enoch Mills. From what I've seen of him he's a good policeman, and he has the authority as undersheriff to investigate anyone who could possibly be Michael Young once I convince him he should. That will take time, and I'm not sure it will help. In the meantime it would be sensible to pack Peggy off to relatives."

Helen was silent. "I can't," she said eventually. "It would be better if we both went somewhere, for a few weeks, however long a time you need to find Michael."

"I'm sorry. You'll have to stay here, Helen."

"What do you mean?" she flared. "Stay and be killed? What kind of sense—"

"If you leave The Shades he's bound to follow, and there's no way I can protect either one of you then. But if you're here it's possible to arrange protection. On second thought, maybe Peggy had better stay; a deputy can keep an eye on her while she's at school without scaring Michael off. I don't want anything to divert his attention from you—and from me."

"What are you going to do?"

"I want to make it clear to Michael that if he tries to harm you in any way he'll have to kill me first." Doremus lighted the miniature cigar he'd been holding. "I think he'll accept the challenge."

"How do you know he'll try to kill you?"

"He'll have to, because I'll be with you twenty-four hours a day from now on." Helen frowned at this piece of news. "Because he's bright, he'll know why I'm sticking close to you and to Peg. Because he's been successful so far, he'll be eager to get on with it, to complete his revenge. I think I understand him well enough to know he won't be worried about me. And one mistake is all he needs to make."

"You're going to stay here?" Helen said, trying not to sound dismayed.

"I'd rather be on the ground floor," Doremus said obliviously.

"I don't think there's room—"

"Your office might be the best place for me; wasn't there some sort of couch in there? Let's have a look." He walked down the unlighted hall with Helen behind him. "What's that—cellar door?" He opened it, peered down the steps, then studied the lock on the door. "No good," he muttered. "Well, I can put a dead bolt lock on in the morning." He closed the door and went on. "That's a bathroom under the stairs, isn't it?"

"Half bath; there's no tub, and the shower isn't very—"

"All I need is a place to shave in the morning," Doremus said cheerfully, turning on the light in the foyer. He stopped in the office doorway and looked down at the clutter. The sofa he had referred to was a Victorian piece about five and a half feet long, rigidly padded.

"Perfect," Doremus said. "No windows; I like that."

"I suppose I could move some things out—"

"No need to go to any trouble; I'll be comfortable here. In the morning if you have time we might run over to my place for a few things."

"You can't sleep on that sofa; it would be like lying on a sidewalk all night."

"I only sleep when there's nothing else to do," Doremus said. "I noticed you had a fine antique chess set in the other room. I'll borrow it for a few nights if you don't mind."

Helen stared at him, hazily. "You're really staying, aren't you?"

"Is something wrong?"

"No. Oh, no."

"Sure I won't be in the way here?"

"We'll . . . we'll manage. Business as usual." Her eyes were stinging from strain. "I'll bring down some bedding and fresh towels for you. Then I think I'll . . . go to bed myself."

"Good idea, get a good night's sleep. Mind if I go up with you?"

"What?"

"I'd like to study the layout of the house."

"Oh." They walked up the stairs slowly; Doremus paused frequently to locate squeaking steps before proceeding. Once they were on the second floor he entered Helen's bedroom without asking, went over to the dormer windows, studied the backyard until he had every tree memorized. Then he opened one of the windows and leaned out, examining the line of the roof. When he was satisfied that the second floor was inaccessible from the ground except by means of a ladder, he closed the window, locked it and drew the blinds.

Helen was pulling linen out of a hall closet when Doremus wandered out of her room. "Where does Peggy sleep?" he whispered. Helen showed him. He walked down the hall, eased Peggy's door open, looked inside. Then he turned to the door opposite the little girl's bedroom.

"My husband's study," Helen said, approaching with an armful of towels and blankets. "Most of his things are still in there, and—"

"I won't disturb anything," Doremus promised, and he went in, his cigar glowing in the dark. Helen sighed and turned the light on for him.

"That's a nice collection of guns," Doremus observed, indicating a tall walnut cabinet near the door.

"My husband was a game warden. Do you like guns?"

"No. But I learned how to live with them." He pointed to a .22-caliber Colt automatic target pistol. "That one ought to do, provided you have ammunition to go with it."

Helen gave him a blank look.

Doremus said patiently, "It'll probably be necessary for me to shoot him if he comes around."

"Do you really believe Michael will come here?"

"I don't know what he's going to do. I only know what I expect him to do. But I could be all wrong, entirely wrong. . . ." He clamped down on his cigar. "We'll have to see," he said vaguely.

Helen opened the glass doors of the cabinet and took the automatic out for him. Then she pulled out the ammunition drawer. "These have been in here for years," she said, looking doubtfully at the boxes of cartridges.

"Doesn't make any difference." Doremus put the automatic inside his belt after checking it over and finding it reasonably clean. He picked up the pile of bedding and towels and went into the hall. "No need for you to go down again, I'll make out all right. Good night, Helen."

He walked on to the stairs while she turned out the light and closed the door to her husband's study. At the stairs Doremus hesitated for a moment, and turned around. "Don't worry," he whispered, as if he felt it was required of him, then continued down.

Don't worry, Helen thought; she went drearily into her own room and prepared for bed.

She had expected to fall asleep immediately but

her thoughts popped like sparks in her mind, memories gruesome and benign intrigued and disturbed her. *Poor Hap, you never meant my sister any harm, I know that.... Michael, did you hate me so very much for what I did? You never said you hated me, why do you want to kill me now?* She could not imagine him as being alive, grown up, murderous. Still lonely. *How lonely you must be, Michael!* She dozed, and her last conscious thoughts were of Doremus. And she felt no sense of worry at all, because he was there in the house with his little cigars and a target pistol and a chessboard to keep him company; it was all right to sleep now.

10

Not long after dawn Amy was half awakened in her bed by the sound of Craig's car outside. She rolled over, eyelids twitching, her hand groping. The part of the bed in which he had slept was still faintly warm. She reached for his pillow, hugged it tightly against her bare breasts, sighed and dropped off to sleep again.

The ringing of the telephone reawakened her.

Amy struggled upright. "Craig?" she said thickly, and then remembered she had heard him leaving. She glanced at the bedside clock; the time was seven-forty-five. "Why didn't you get me up?" she said crossly. The phone rang again. Amy popped her eardrums with a yawn, shuddered, reached for the receiver of the telephone.

"H'lo?"

"I want to talk to Craig."

"What?"

"Let me talk to Craig," the boy repeated.

"Craig . . ." Amy said, trying to get her bearing. "Craig isn't . . . it's eight o'clock in the morning; what makes you think he'd be here? Who is this, please?"

"He *was* there," the voice said deliberately. "He was sleeping right there with you. Where did he go?"

"Are you calling from the school?" Amy felt a chill that gripped her like jaws. "Who are you?"

"Michael," he said emphatically, without hesitation, "and I want—"

"Michael?"

". . . to talk to Craig."

"Michael Young?" There was no sound on the line for several seconds. Amy felt as if she'd swallowed her tongue when she tried to speak. "What . . . Why do you want Craig?"

"I have to tell him something," the boy said with great impatience.

"He . . . he really isn't here. I mean it, he left. I was half asleep, but I heard him drive away." Having admitted that much, Amy lost some of her shock and became cautious, realizing that she might be talking to one of the more Machiavellian Greenleaf boys. She said boldly, "Prove you're Michael Young." The silence that followed was so long she was afraid he was going to hang up. But eventually he spoke again, in a voice that was mischievous, but with an underlying hint of malice.

"When my mother was a little girl, she was playing with Auntie Helen. They called their game 'beauty shop.' My mother cut all of Auntie Helen's hair off with scissors. It was red hair when she cut it, but when the hair grew out it changed color, to dark brown. Auntie Helen knows. Ask her."

140

"All right. That's ... a good story, if it's true, and I will ask Helen." Amy was already certain that he had told the truth; she was now certain that this was Michael Young. "But do you have any more proof?"

"I don't want to talk to you any more," he said.

"Last night ... something bad happened to Sheriff Washbrook. Do you know anything about it?"

"I know," Michael said, his voice sullen.

"Were you there?"

"He got what he had coming. Would you put Craig on?"

Amy said desperately, "Michael, where are you now? I'd like to come and see you."

"I told you, I *don't* want to talk to you!" Michael cried.

"Please listen to me. Craig isn't here. But if there's something you want to tell him, then tell me, and I'll find him right away."

Amy thought she had demanded too much, but then he said, in a voice that seemed to be fading, "Tell him ... I wish he was dead."

"Oh, no. No, Michael. You don't mean that."

"I wish he was dead. I hate him."

"You can't hate everyone, Michael. You just can't! Craig was good to you, he took care of you. . . ." She caught her breath, and listened incredulously. He was weeping. "Michael," Amy continued, "I do want to help you. Please tell me where you are, and I'll come right away."

He sobbed again. "I'm—" he started to say, and then the connection was broken.

Amy sat holding the receiver with her knees almost against her breasts, and she was shivering. Presently she became aware of tears running

141

down her cheeks. She dried them with the hem of the bedsheet and replaced the receiver. Despite the sun at the windows the room seemed cold to her. She slipped out of bed, took a heavy robe from her closet and put it on. A cigarette helped calm her. She went to the telephone again, began dialing Craig's number, changed her mind before she finished and bowed her head.

"Oh, God, what am I going to *do*?" Amy said brokenly, but she'd already half made up her mind, so she finished her cigarette and dressed hurriedly, in slacks and a ski sweater, and, forgetting about work, she went out into the chilly mist-bright morning to the ramshackle garage for her car.

Doremus asked her to go over the telephone conversation with Michael four times, until he was satisfied that he had it nearly word for word. When Helen left them alone in the kitchen to greet an early-rising antique hound Doremus asked bluntly, "Why did he call your house looking for Craig?" Amy reddened. "Oh well, what time did Craig leave, then?"

"I don't know," Amy mumbled. "It was light outside. He might have left as early as six-thirty, or as late as seven-thirty. I heard his car, but I didn't really wake up."

Helen came back and poured fresh coffee for the three of them. "How are we going to tell Craig?" she asked.

Doremus said, "I don't think he should be told."

"But Michael threatened to kill him!" Amy protested.

"No, he didn't. Not according to what you told

me. Michael said, 'Tell him I wish he was dead.' That isn't a threat."

"As far as *I'm* concerned it is. And he also said he hated Craig."

"Supposing he does."

"Well, doesn't that mean he intends—"

Doremus shook his head. "I don't know why he called you; it wasn't what I expected. But what Michael had to say doesn't change my mind about him. I still believe he intends to murder Helen next."

Amy almost dropped her coffee cup and she gave Helen a startled look. Helen smiled wanly and explained while Doremus industriously buttered half a pastry and ate it.

"Michael's alive?" Amy said, staring at Doremus. "Well, now, if you'll pardon my saying so, *that's* incredible."

" 'Ghosties and beasties and things that go bump in the night' you believe in, but a rational explanation defeats you."

"Rational, ha! Your 'explanation' simply explains away too much. What about the little boy everyone has seen? Peggy saw him twice, and poor Elsa. . . . Also, I talked to a boy on the telephone this morning, not a man."

"A man mimicking a ten-year-old boy," Doremus suggested.

"No, sir," Amy said stubbornly. "I work with boys that age, I listen to them eight or ten hours a day. I'm not about to be fooled by an impersonation. The voice I heard was genuine."

Helen nodded. "I agree with Amy. I don't know if we heard the same voice, but I'm convinced—"

"Anyone can be fooled over the telephone," Doremus objected.

"I asked him to prove he was Michael Young," Amy said, "and he did."

Doremus looked at her with renewed interest. "Something you forgot to tell me?"

"Yes. After I asked him to give me proof there was a long silence, and then he said, in a sort of smart-alecky way—you know how they are at that age—oh, God! he said that when Helen and her sister were little girls they liked to play 'beauty shop.' Beauty shop. And one time Alice took a pair of scissors and cut almost all of Helen's hair off. Her hair had been red, but when it grew back it had changed color, to dark brown."

An odd expression crossed Helen's face. "That's perfectly true. My parents made a terrible fuss about the hair-cutting although it didn't matter very much to me. Alice was delighted, I think—there was always this rivalry between us. But I doubt if I've ever told anyone about that incident."

"Alice must have told the boys," Amy said, and turned to Doremus. "Well, what do you think about that?"

Doremus grinned broadly. "I'll stick by my theories," he said, sipping from his cup. "Now, this is just about right, Helen. It took me thirty years to learn how to make coffee this way, but you're catching on fast."

"That's good," Helen said dryly, with a glance at Amy. "Doremus cooked breakfast for us this morning."

"Oh, won't Brenda be thrilled to have another cook in the house?"

Doremus grinned again, and unwrapped a small cigar.

144

"How long do you think you'll have to stay here?" Amy asked him.

"No telling."

"Couldn't a deputy watch the house, keep an eye on Helen and Peggy?"

"Not as well as I can," Doremus said.

"In the meantime Craig's life is in danger, and you don't seem to think a thing about it."

"Somehow I don't," Doremus admitted. "I could be mistaken though."

"You mean you just might admit your reckoning was off—over Craig's dead body you might admit it."

"Amy," Helen murmured.

"I can't keep still about it, I *have* to tell Craig about Michael." She faltered. "I could use some help."

"Why don't you ask him over tonight?" Doremus said to both women. "We can bring him up to date and at the least he ought to know what I'm doing here, what I'm after. He might have some valuable suggestions." Doremus yawned and stood up. "Believe I'll put in a call to Enoch Mills; I want to see if they've found anything of interest up at the state park." He sauntered away, cigar in hand, unshaven and looking thoroughly at home.

"I don't know what to think about that man," Amy said in a low voice. "As late as last night I was sure he had possibilities, but he's ... well, he's on the boorish side, isn't he?"

"I don't know," Helen said vacantly.

"I thought you might be getting interested in him."

Helen smiled bleakly. "I may be turned upside down these days, but I haven't taken leave of my senses."

"Good. Because I've definitely decided he's not for you. Still ..." Amy stirred a lump of sugar into her cooling coffee. "He's not thoughtful, and he's awfully presumptuous in some ways, but there's something about him. Children certainly notice it right away. They can't be fooled."

"No, they always respond to kindness," Helen said.

Craig came that night and listened stonily as Amy repeated the details of the telephone call from Michael. To her dismay he said nothing but looked at her as if she were lying, or losing her mind. Then Doremus took over and explained that he thought Michael was still alive. Craig was immediately interested, and unargumentative. He asked a great many questions, becoming more excited by the minute, so much so that he got up and began pacing restlessly the length of the kitchen.

"That's it," he muttered. "That has to be what happened! Michael lived through the blizzard. I'll start checking our records tonight to see if there was a boy missing from the school about the time my brother disappeared. Have you asked Enoch Mills to go through the sheriff's files on missing persons?"

Doremus nodded. "Mills drew a blank, but that isn't necessarily significant. Missing children often go unreported."

"Maybe Michael did survive," Amy said sharply to Doremus, not caring what Craig would think, "but there's still a little boy involved in all this. I don't see how you can deny that, or ignore it!"

Amy had halfway made up her mind that Doremus was a bumbler, and she wasn't prepared for the look he gave her. His eyes had a wolfish glint in them. Amy was suddenly aware of a formidable strength in this man which she had previously overlooked. She was, despite herself, intrigued by her discovery.

"I haven't ignored anything," he said quietly, "but for now all I can do is wait. And hope I haven't made any serious mistakes in judgment."

About two o'clock in the morning Helen came wide awake in her bed, icily certain that her room had been entered.

The sky outside was veiled with clouds and heavily tarnished by the yellow moon; the shadow of a tree loomed mothlike on one wall of the room. She saw a gliding figure near the bed and almost cried out.

"Mother," Peggy said plaintively, "I don't feel very good. I've got a stomachache."

Helen let her breath out a notch at a time and got up to help her daughter. She was wide awake by the time she returned to her room. The thought of strong hot coffee pushed her back into the hall.

Helen had thought it might be possible to sneak downstairs and invade the kitchen without being detected by Doremus; she was halfway down the stairs without having made a sound at all, as far as she knew, when the door of the office opened and Doremus stepped out, pistol in hand. The high-intensity lamp behind him was masked, revealing only the square battlefield of the chessboard he had been studying.

"Could you make enough for two?" he asked her.

When the coffee was ready Helen carried it to the office on a tray. He was hunched over the ornately manned chessboard again; the black Colt pistol was only inches away from his left hand.

"Are you playing yourself?" Helen asked.

"No. These are my men here. Black belongs to a man named Arshenko, a Russian philologist at the Moscow University. We've been playing for years, ever since I met him at the University of Chicago. Play by mail now. I've only beaten him once in four years, but I think ... I've got him now. I should know by next spring." He looked up, accepting a cup of the steaming coffee. "I don't suppose you play?"

"My husband and I used to play once in a while, but I—"

"Great!" Doremus enthused, sweeping the pieces from the board. "Would you care for a game right now?"

"What about Mr. Arshenko?"

"He can wait; I still have three days to decide on my next move." He began setting up the game. Helen thought of her bed upstairs, and sighed inaudibly. "I suppose one game ... I'm really not very expert at this."

She proved it by losing to him within twenty minutes. Doremus then went over every mistake she had made in painstaking detail. Eventually a yawn burst out of her. Doremus looked in amazement at the clock on the desk.

"You really did very well," he said. "I think you have an aptitude for this game. My wife never could learn...." He reached for a cigar, discovered he had smoked the last one and sat back, staring disconsolately at the chessboard. Helen was putting the coffee cups back on the serving tray and she glanced at him, then felt moved to ask:

"When did your wife die, Doremus?"

"Three years ago."

"Her name was Marian."

"Yes. That's right." He was silent, but he looked up at Helen thoughtfully. "You've put up with this very well, my moving in and all. I know it hasn't been easy for you. But there's no other way. I have to be here."

"I understand."

"He might not come . . . but if he does, you wouldn't have a chance alone. Marian never had a chance. She put up a fight, but what chance did she have?" His expression was cold, brooding.

Helen felt shocked by his words, but she couldn't make herself ask Doremus what had happened to his wife. His tension lessened, however, and he began to speak again.

"I had to fly out to Des Moines to bring back a suspect in a labor shooting. Usually when I was to be away overnight Marian drove to my sister's and stayed with them, but she was helping with a neighbor's wedding and she felt that she couldn't leave. She felt safe enough, and with reason: it was a fine spring week and the neighborhood was a good one, but is any neighborhood good enough?

"We landed at Meigs Field at four in the morning and it was six by the time I booked my prisoner, almost seven when I reached home. The milkman and I arrived about the same time, so I put the milk in the refrigerator and glanced at the front page of the *Tribune* before going upstairs. There was no sign of forced entry—I would have noticed—the house was just as it should be. So I wasn't prepared at all, I just walked in on it." His eyes stung him; he rubbed them before continuing. "What struck me first was the quantity of blood on the walls; it still seemed fresh, I suppose. The room was devastated. I found Marian behind the bed, I mean jammed between the headboard and the wall. He'd finally broke the blade of his knife after stabbing her half a hundred times."

Helen, in the doorway, had turned a dull shade of gray, but her eyes were wide and filled with pity for him.

Doremus, hardly aware of her, went on inexorably. "The kid was in the bathroom; that was as far as he'd been able to travel. I don't know what she fought back with, fought the knife with, but I'd taught her the use of her hands and feet, I'd taught her a few alley things, and she had courage. He was a neighborhood kid we'd both tried to help. Probably she'd opened the door to him— that's the only explanation I have to this day. He was on the floor of the bathroom because he couldn't walk at all. Some of the blood on the walls was his. He had a scalp-rip and one empty eyesocket, reamed out, no expression on his face, it was hard and stiff like a mask, about an eighth of an inch of coagulated blood covered most of his face but he was conscious and breathing and he could talk. He cursed me when I walked in. I didn't think about what I was doing, or what I wanted to do. I just took out my service revolver and shot him five or six times and walked out again."

Helen could find nothing adequate to say; she took the tray to the kitchen, washed the cups and saucers, put everything away and then returned. Doremus was methodically aligning pieces on the chessboard again. He looked up with a strained smile.

"I didn't mean to bother you with all that."

"When have you had the chance to talk about it?"

"I don't think I've talked about it at all. I didn't know I could."

"You've kept to yourself much too long," Helen said reprovingly. They looked at each other for several moments, cautiously, almost friends. Then Doremus smiled again and reached for his glasses. "I enjoyed the coffee. Maybe we'll have a chance for another game of chess."

"Yes, I'd like that. Doremus ... I'm afraid I haven't been particularly gracious the last couple of days. I apologize for that. I'm glad you're here, very glad. And not just because of Michael. I hope when this is over with, you'll feel like coming back for an evening now and then."

"Peg offered me half of her allowance if I'd stay on permanently," Doremus said innocently, and Helen, after turning red, laughed with him.

"She would. Good night, Doremus."

11

Long past midnight he drove west through the sleeping village and up the long grade of White Church Street, past the widely spaced and darkened houses. There was no moon; he had waited far longer than he cared to wait for a moonless night, but now that the time had come he felt no sense of hurry, no spoiling overeagerness. He had gone over it in his mind again and again, timing himself from the one quick rehearsal he'd managed a week before. He knew he should be into the house, and out again, within twenty minutes. Out again, and on his way. A long way off by daybreak. That, of course, was essential.

When he was almost opposite the Connelly house, Harry steered off onto the hard shoulder on the far side of the road, parking beneath some high sycamore trees. While he studied the house he let the engine idle. The last two blocks he had driven only with parking lights. Now he turned off all lights and the engine but continued to sit for several minutes longer, observing, trying not to look directly at the street light that illuminated part of the front yard beyond the stone fence.

As soon as he became conscious of his heartbeat and felt his palms getting coldly wet, Harry knew that it was time to go. He took the items he needed from the seat beside him. The laundry sack with the drawstring top went up under his black sweater. The thick-bodied jackknife he slipped into his right-hand pants pocket. Switchblade knives were more convenient, but even with the good ones you couldn't trust the blade not to snap.

Harry eased open the door of his car and got out, was motionless for a few seconds, his quick breath visible like steam in the dark. Then he crossed the street without haste, hearing a dog start up somewhere; he scarcely paid attention.

Beyond the range of the street light he paused once again before stepping over the low wall that surrounded the Connelly property. Once in the yard he felt safer, and he went more quickly. The yard had been thoroughly raked the day before and a leaf crackled only once in a while under his shoes. His path was clear and familiar. He knew every contour of the big yard.

For the third time he stopped, this time close to the side of the house, caught his breath there and had a good look around. From where he was standing Harry couldn't make out his car. The street was still empty. No one had driven past.

He took the big jackknife out of his pocket and opened the five-inch blade. As he walked toward the side porch he held the blade down, near his right leg, so there could be no unexpected reflections of light. The weight of the knife in his hand was a small comfort, though he didn't feel particularly worried. He knew how it would go inside.

The door of the porch was three steps above him. Nothing but glass in the door, he thought, with a touch of contempt. Even if he hadn't learned about the malfunctioning lock it would have been no trouble to get in . . . might have taken him a little longer.

With the blade of his knife and a proper amount of pressure brought to bear on the weak lock at the right time, the door was open. Nothing to it. He was in, with hardly a sound. Just a quick snap.

He thought of the woman asleep in her bed and for an instant he grinned, and wondered how it would be to wake her, to see the expression on her face. But that was not what he had come for. Harry felt a little sorry.

The porch was so cluttered with cases and cabinets and "junk"—as he thought of it—that he was forced to feel his way step by step to the more spacious living room. He had decided it would be all right to use his light once he was inside the house, but now, for some reason, he hesitated to do so. By that time his night vision had improved considerably. He knew where he was going. Better not risk a light until it was necessary.

Halfway through the living room he stopped to slow down his rate of breathing and to do some listening, but he was now impatient to finish and so he went on while blood was still throbbing in his temples. Because of diffused light from the street, the foyer was faintly visible. He could make out the curved railing of the stairway, and the two display cases against the front wall, next to the door.

It seemed to him that he could smell cigar smoke, which puzzled him. But it wasn't a strong odor. Hours old, he thought, and shifted his attention to the display cases, drawing one hand lightly over a glass surface. He touched the small lock. He could almost open it with his little finger, Harry thought. Why bother to have a lock at all if—

The foyer was suddenly filled with a shocking, glaring light that came from behind him, like a photographic flash, and Harry froze completely with both hands atop the case. But the light didn't vanish immediately, as it should have, instead, it seemed to be pushing through the back of his head.

"Stay just like that," Doremus cautioned. "Move a finger and I'll put a bullet through the back of your knee, Michael."

The opened knife was lying only a few inches from the spread fingers of his right hand. He glanced at the knife, hesitated, slid his hand a fraction toward it.

"I mean what I say. Now take a step back and turn around—but be careful."

There was no nervousness in the voice and no lack of authority, so Harry gave up and turned slowly, shielding his eyes from the potent light.

"OK, OK, you're blinding me!"

"Stand still!" Doremus moved sideways in the direction of the stairs, placed the 80,000 candle-power light on the Sheraton table, where it continued to envelop Harry Randle, and dialed a telephone number with one hand. After the phone had rung half a dozen times he said sharply, "Enoch? Sorry to get you up this time of night, but I've got him. . . . That's right, Michael Young."

155

"What?" Harry said, scowling.

"In the house; I think he was on his way upstairs." He listened for a few seconds. "Good. I'll meet you at your office, then."

"What the hell . . ."

"Shut up," Doremus said with a look of loathing at the knife.

"Who's Michael Young? You mean that kid who—"

Doremus turned on the foyer light and glanced up the steps as Helen Connelly appeared. She looked from Doremus to Harry Randle, and then at the Colt automatic Doremus was holding. "What's the matter? Why is Harry—"

"Say hello to your Aunt Helen," Doremus instructed Harry.

"Mrs. Connelly, is this guy crazy?"

Helen just stared at them both, baffled. And then she ventured a closer look at Harry Randle, who stared back, sullen and a little frightened.

"But Doremus . . . how could . . . are you sure . . . ?"

"I'm sure he went to the trouble to break in here tonight. I'm sure he came with that knife there."

"Listen," Harry said, rather desperately, "My name's Randle. *Randle*. I never heard of any Michael Young until Doc Britton—" A look of dismay came into Harry's eyes, and he studied Doremus incredulously. "What's going on here? Are you trying to . . . What do you keep calling me *Michael* for?"

"Because I think you are Michael Young. And you came here tonight to kill Helen."

"God!" Harry said, and seemed on the verge of bolting for the nearest door.

"I can fire twice for every step you take," Doremus reminded him. "This may be just a twenty-two, but I guarantee you'll gain some weight in a hurry if you try a break."

"God!" Harry said again, almost collapsing, and he looked as pale as a night moth. He licked his lips and gestured with one hand and then said quickly, "I was on my way out of town—I was leaving this place for good! That's why . . . I got the idea a long time ago. Hauling furniture around in here I had a chance to look over most of the good stuff she has—you know, all this jewelry here—and I figured . . . figured when the time came to move on I'd sort of stop off here first and load up. I've got a laundry sack under this sweater, see for yourself; I knew it wouldn't take me five minutes to fill it up, and I thought I could unload the stuff later on for a few hundred." He looked at Helen and seemed to be embarrassed momentarily, but then he glanced at Doremus, beseechingly. He pulled at his sweater and the laundry sack plopped to the floor.

"There! See! I'm telling you the truth! My car's right across the street. The lock on the porch there is bad, it wasn't any work getting inside, just had to use the blade of my knife—but I didn't come to kill anybody! I don't even know her except to work for! Mister, my name's Harry Randle. Harry! Randle!"

"Calm down, you'll wake Peggy," Doremus said, and as he considered Harry's defense of himself he began to have his first, instinctive, cop-wise doubts.

"I'll put some coffee on," Helen murmured, because it was the only thing she could think of. She glided down the stairs, past Doremus with another searching apprehensive look at Randle.

"You'll find out," Harry said darkly. "I'm not

lying to you. You'll find out who I am. You're not making me out a killer."

"You're right about one thing anyway. In the next twenty-four hours we're going to learn more about you than you know yourself. Ever take a polygraph test, Randle?"

"No," Harry said, after a long moment. "But I don't have anything against taking it. I don't have anything to hide."

They both heard the sheriff's patrol car pull up outside and Harry looked back over one shoulder, convulsively. Doremus had the notion he might try to run after all. But then Harry's shoulders drooped and he waited broodingly, eyes on the floor, until the deputies came to collect him.

Enoch Mills, the undersheriff of Shades County, was a tall, powerfully built man with half his hair, sloping shoulders and ingenuous freckles around his normally placid, cool green eyes. Although Doremus hadn't known him long, he was aware that Mills was a competent policeman whose chief trait was thoroughness and who had the ability to work well with, and get the most out of, many types of men.

Mills quickly secured the cooperation of the Highway Patrol in investigating the background of Harry Randle. Taking turns with Doremus, he questioned Harry until the young thief was groggy and speechless. As Doremus had promised, by six o'clock the following evening they had learned more about Harry than Harry knew himself. And they had proved to themselves that Harry Randle was nobody but Harry Randle after all, orphanage raised, street toughened, prison bred. The polygraph established that he was not a murderer, and he had not been anywhere near the scene of the shooting of Hap Washbrook.

"Too bad he didn't turn out to be Michael Young," Mills said in his office as they were relaxing over acrid cups of restaurant coffee. "I liked your theory, Doremus. Now we're back to a lot of . . . well, we're back to ghosts, and things like that, and at least one murder hanging over our heads."

"It's still a good theory, even if Harry was the wrong man," Doremus said stubbornly. "I don't think we can afford to let down now. If we didn't get Michael Young, then he's still around somewhere, waiting for his chance. Maybe he'll come tomorrow night." Doremus rubbed his tiring eyes. "Or maybe he won't."

"Well, you could have it worse. I hear Mrs. Connelly is a right fine cook."

Doremus grinned. "Oh, I don't know. I think I'm better."

12

Although Doremus was considerably less trouble than the average house guest, Helen soon discovered that having a full-time bodyguard and watchman was a strain on her nerves. By Saturday she was ready to jump at any excuse to get out of the house for a couple of hours, without Doremus tagging along; a PTA get-together at The Shades School seemed to offer a perfect opportunity, but she had to argue for almost an hour before Doremus grudgingly conceded she ought to be safe there without him.

"It's in the gym; there'll be three hundred people there!"

"That's what I don't like about it."

"One of them could be Michael, is that what you're thinking? He wouldn't dare try anything."

Doremus looked gloomily at the stub of his cigar. "I said you could go. Keep Peggy with you at all times."

"Of course I will."

"Park your car as close to the gym as you can, and it would be a good idea if you asked one of your friends to follow you home after the party; you don't have to explain why."

"All right," Helen said resignedly, wondering if she was going to enjoy her night out as much as she had anticipated.

"Call me if—"

"You remind me of my father!"

"I'll shut up," Doremus said, with a sardonic grin.

With the house to himself, Doremus took a leisurely hot shower, put on fresh Levi's and a favorite Pendleton shirt and walked outside. The night was just cool enough for a heavy accumulation of ground mist: the light of the village center four blocks away looked nebulous and there were belt-high pockets of mist in the sloping backyard. He strolled around the house, paused for a time by the thick trunk of a hickory, blended with the trunk. A cat came out of the mist, hurrying; it stopped, looked the way it had come, and trotted on. Doremus waited to see what else might be coming out of the mist.

After five minutes or so he became convinced that he was alone, and so he returned to the house, turned off the porch light and settled down in the office with an exemplary western novel. He was thoroughly absorbed in the fortunes of the Zachary family when the telephone rang.

Doremus looked up without much interest, then went back to *The Unforgiven*. The phone continued ringing. When he counted eight rings Doremus put the book down and rose. By the tenth ring he was certain that whoever was calling expected him to answer.

"Connellys'," he said gruffly.

"You want to see me, don't you?"

Several seconds passed before Doremus answered; there was a chilly grin on his face. "That's right, kid."

"You can see me half an hour from now at the gristmill on Hawke's farm."

"Half hour. Is that when you materialize, or whatever it is you do?"

"And you'd better come alone, or you won't see me."

The connection was broken, before Doremus could think of some way to keep him talking. He replaced the receiver and looked thoughtfully at his wristwatch. The time was a few minutes after nine. The boy had spoken quickly and sharply, as if he were as tired of waiting for a confrontation as Doremus himself. "That old gristmill?" Doremus said, half-aloud. "Don't you think you're stacking the odds, kid?" He reached for the telephone again, and dialed the home of Enoch Mills.

"This is Doremus," he said, when he had the undersheriff of The Shades on the line. "I just heard from Michael Young." He remembered then that the boy had not identified himself, but he went on: "I'm being set up for something, but I'm not sure what. . . . Yes, I probably could use some help. Helen Connelly took Peggy to some sort of school affair about an hour ago; I think it would be smart to send one of your deputies down there to keep an eye on her, without attracting a lot of attention. Now, I'm supposed to be at the gristmill on Hawke's farm in . . . approximately twenty-five minutes, and I'll be there all right. No, I don't want that. Give me, say, an hour, and then come in full throttle. I can stay alive that long no matter what, and I want him to feel secure enough to show himself."

The gristmill on Ironwall Creek had been built in the 1840's and was still operable, although it now served primarily as an out-of-the-way attraction for tourists with cameras looking for picturesque antiquities, and as a subject for local painters. It was located a hundred feet upstream from an unpaved farm road and at night was all but invisible, surrounded by massed trees at the water's edge.

Doremus had visited the area on several occasions, casting for bronze-backer in the weedy waters of the creek, and he remembered the high-walled, slightly out-of-kilter building well. There was an easy downhill approach from the pasture on the north side of the mill. He could see moonlit mist on the broad pasture through the ranks of trees at the water's edge. And there was a more difficult approach, beginning at the foot of the bridge, continuing below the steep bank. He had chosen this path, not for secrecy—anyone with half an ear could hear his motor scooter for miles on a still night—but because it offered maximum concealment until he was ready to show himself.

After pulling his scooter off the road Doremus found a creekside path with the beam of his flashlight and started toward the mill. In his left hand he carried the nine-shot automatic.

Buckbrush slowed him down, but he was not overanxious to begin with. When he was sure he could find his way without falling into the water, he continued without a light until the mill wheel rose above him. There he paused, listening to the mill race, studying the packed-earth clearing in front of the mill entrance. Distantly the hilly pasture shimmered, faintly yellow. There was moonlight enough to show him the heights and angles of the mill, the boarded upper windows. He clipped the lightweight lamp to his belt and climbed up the slope, keeping low. Then he drew a breath, dashed for the doorway, kneeled there, pressed against the wall.

There was a padlock on the door but it hung oddly from the hasp, as if sheared by bolt cutters. Doremus, feeling cold and naked in the clearing, lifted one foot and kicked the door in. A moment later he went inside like a snake, rolled clear of the visible doorway, rose to his knees in the protective blackness, his lungs aching, his hands steady. He could see nothing at all. The mill smelled old, it smelled like rotting grain and rats. He moved cautiously and silently to his right.

Somewhere in the darkness a child giggled, muffling the sound with his hands, or his sleeve. Doremus froze, his thumb on the push button of the flashlight.

"All right," he said, not loudly, "I'm ready to talk, and I'd like to see you." He moved again, swiftly this time, on hands and knees. There was no flooring, at least where he was. He heard a tentative scurrying close by, in the loose dirt, but ignored it. He was listening for the sound of something human.

The child giggled again, openly, delightedly.

Doremus scrambled up, switching on the full beam of the light. The beam traveled in a wide blinding arc, past rough cut wooden columns, over a grinding stone, and pinned the sneaker-clad boy on the landing of a flight of stairs.

The startled boy lifted his hands, trying to shut out the glare, which was equal to that of a locomotive's headlight at short range. Doremus shielded his own eyes with an upthrust arm and began closing in. But the boy recovered quickly, turned his back and bounded up the stairs, too fast for Doremus, who tried to track him with the light.

At the foot of the stairs, Doremus stopped, aimed the beam upward. He heard no sound, but dust was drifting down, as if someone was walking cautiously just above.

"Michael!"

He began climbing, pausing on every other step. The light was a powerful weapon, but he had lost his advantage and knew it. The sight of the boy had astonished him; he had expected almost anything else. . . . "I don't want to play games, Michael!" Doremus called. "I just want to talk to you." He reached the landing, where the stairs made a sharp angle to the left. Here the advantage became Michael's. But there was no choice except to go on.

He was halfway to the second floor of the mill when the heavy pitchfork came down, almost straight down, dropped but apparently not thrown. It struck Doremus' right wrist, and he let go of the light. He was not quick enough to seize the light before it fell through a space between steps and dropped to the ground below. Doremus recovered and fired three shots in a random pattern, intended to frighten and not to wound the boy he was chasing. Then he stumbled up on the last of the steps in the dark, ran into a wall, stopped there and waited, breathing harshly.

"Your turn," he said, when he had caught his breath.

The boy giggled, sounding a little short of breath himself.

Doremus flexed the fingers of his right hand, reached into the pocket of his shirt and withdrew a pencil flashlight. He heard the giggling again; this time the boy seemed closer, but the sound was muffled and it was impossible to be certain. Doremus was tempted to use the tiny light immediately, but he had no more surprises to offer and he didn't want to waste that one.

While he waited his eyes adjusted to the dark. A little moonlight seemed to be filtering in, perhaps through cracks in the roof or the plank walls. Doremus edged forward, fingertips on the rough wall. The floor under his feet creaked and he stopped. A few seconds later the floor creaked again, but not from his weight. He reached out with his right hand; the wall ended, and there was a space. He felt a chill at the nape of his neck. Door space? he wondered. Was there a room beyond, and was the boy hiding there? He thought about the pitchfork that had come heavily down inches from his head, and he suppressed a shudder. But he took no more time to consider the possible danger; instead he switched on the pencil flashlight, stepped boldly into the space and pointed the beam.

The boy was standing about ten feet away, and for two or three seconds he was mesmerized by the light, his mouth open, a dull puzzled gleam in his eyes. Then he bolted, and vanished.

Doremus shifted the automatic to his right hand and made a blind lunge for the boy, grasping the sleeve of his coat momentarily. But the boy twisted free; in the next instant Doremus was hit solidly in the back of the head and he pitched forward to the floor, stunned.

Now what the hell? he thought, and tried to get up, but only his mind was working—working him up into a panic. He had no idea whether he was still holding onto the automatic, but he tried to roll over on his back. The effort caused him to lose consciousness for several seconds. He awoke with a sickening pain in his skull, feeling helpless and condemned. Somewhere there was movement. Instinctively he sought to protect himself: he turned his head and raised an arm as a searing liquid poured down, soaking him to his toes. The fumes in his nostrils had the effect of ammonia.

Gasoline, he thought, groping, trying to balance himself on his feet. *Gasoline!* He coughed and struggled to keep his dripping hands away from his eyes, which had begun to burn frightfully from the fumes and from the gasoline trickling down his forehead. He groaned aloud.

There was a wavering, orange-yellow light outside the room, showing him the location of the doorway. Doremus, seeing the opening dimly, plunged toward it. Then he stopped in horror.

Michael stood outside, facing him impassively. He held a burning torch in one hand.

Doremus retreated instantly, clawing at the buttons of his sodden shirt. When he failed in his efforts to unbutton the shirt he tore it from his body. But the gasoline was still wet on his skin, it singed his sink delicately and suggestively.

"Now listen, boy," he said, backing away, "you're going to burn us both up with that thing. Don't come any closer." Michael seemed not to hear. He advanced carefully, a step at a time, his eyes solemn.

"Damn it, the fumes will ignite!" Doremus yelled, still retreating. "Now put that torch out, stomp it out quick, you hear me!" He could feel the wall behind his back and he edged sideways. Michael hesitated, seeming mildly uncertain about what he was doing. Then he smiled and came on, more quickly, holding out the torch. His lips trembled, as if he were trying to speak.

Doremus threw himself back against the wall, since there was no place else for him to go. The torch was close enough for him to feel the heat of it.

"No!" he shouted.

Behind him dry boards splintered and popped like firecrackers, giving way; he toppled out of range of the burning curling torch in the boy's hand, and cried out fearfully, shocked by weightlessness, by a rush of cold air. The side of the gristmill appeared to leap away from him, recede into darkness. Doremus had a confused impression of sky and circling trees and then, luckily for him, he plunged head down into the placid waters of the mill-pond.

By the time he managed to paddle ashore, covered with slime and still redolent of gasoline, he was exhausted and shaking. He lay in the weeds and leaves for several minutes, half unconscious, until he heard voices. Then he made the necessary effort to pull himself all the way out of the water. Trembling and sick to his stomach, he staggered and crawled as far as the clearing in front of the mill, where a light flashed on him.

"Just hold it right where you are, mister, we've got two shotguns here!"

"Did you see him?" Doremus mumbled. "Is he still in there? Where's the boy?"

"He sure is a mess. Get a whiff of him, Pa. Is that gasoline I smell?"

"Messing around my mill with gasoline, mister?" the older Hawke said threateningly.

A third man came crashing through the buckbrush. "What have you got here, Pa?"

"Just some crazy old bum, Willis," Hawke muttered. "All right, you get walking."

"I'm trying to explain," said Doremus, standing his ground, "that there was a little boy here just a few minutes ago. *He's* the one who tried to set fire to your mill . . . set fire to me too. He's about ten years old; dark hair, fair skin. He was wearing sneakers. I don't know where he went but we've got to find him!"

"Pa," one of the boys shouted, "looks like that bum fell through a winda round back. There's boards swimming in the pond."

The other son scratched his cheek and said to Doremus, "A little boy, huh?"

"That's right, did you see him?"

"Coulda been a little boy I saw hightailing across the meadow two-three minutes ago. Didn't get a good look."

"Which way was he headed?" Doremus asked eagerly.

"North. Toward the Overmeyers' place. Pa, you figure there's any truth in what he's saying?"

Doremus explained who he was, naming Enoch Mills as a reference, and Mr. Hawke seemed a little less inclined to give him both barrels on the spot. "Well," he drawled. "I guess it won't hurt to go along with you far as the Overmeyers'. Jack, you and Willis look in the mill, see if there was

169

any damage done. Willis, give this man your jacket so he don't freeze to death."

"It's my new jacket, Pa."

He ain't gonna steal it. Come with me, mister, and you two watch out for yourselves."

Gratefully buttoning up the fleece-lined jacket he had borrowed, Doremus followed the farmer, who had a light of the type Doremus had taken with him into the barn. They made good time to the crest of the meadow, and there, in full moonlight, they paused to study the landscape. There was not even a cow in sight.

"That's the Overmeyer place," Hawke said pointing.

"Who owns the property down by the road there?"

"Man named Brunell. Artist of some sort; don't know him well." He turned toward the Overmeyer farm. "Reckon this the way we ought to go, but it don't seem like much use."

"Why not split up?" Doremus suggested. "The boy might have headed toward Brunell's; there are a lot of trees for cover down there."

"Yehp, but if he knows this pasture he wouldn't have run that way—gets real marshy for about fifty yards below that old barn."

"He might not know the pasture though. I think I'll have a look at Brunell's. Borrow your light?"

"What? Oh, take it, otherwise you'll have mud all over Willis' good jacket. Mister, I hope this is worth all the trouble."

"It's worth it," Doremus said, and he started rapidly down the slope of the pasture while Hawke walked off toward the other farm. With the powerful light it was easy for Doremus to avoid the worst of the marsh when he came to it, and once he had crossed the marsh he found easy going to the big peaked barn above.

The property seemed deserted. There was a light in the small house a hundred yards away, close to the road, but no dogs came barking and no animals stomped restlessly in the barn at his approach. Looking up, Doremus had an inkling why. There was a large skylight, facing north, on one wing of the roof.

He killed his light and moved closer to the barn, staying in shadow. The great front doors of the barn were securely chained shut, but there was a sign next to them. Doremus masked his light with his hand and turned it on the sign. BRUNELL GALLERIES, it said. PLEASE ENTER AT THE BACK.

Doremus looked over one shoulder at the house. For an instant he saw someone silhouetted in the single lighted window. Near the house the woods were thick, a likely hiding place, if Michael had come this way. Chances were he was half a mile gone by now, gaining all the time. . . .

Inside the barn there was a spate of noise, a curious, flat, metallic clashing.

Doremus slipped around to the side of the barn and walked past small darkened windows, a dozen or more, until he reached a conventional door with flagstones in front of it. There was another sign but he didn't stop to ponder it, because the door was standing open. He opened it a little more and stepped inside, switching on the flashlight as he did so. The first thing he saw was an enormous, seal-like bronze nude on a granite pedestal four feet high. Behind her there were other seals—or women, but what they were wasn't immediately apparent—and then a spindly forest of cold-steel men, some walking, some running, some kneeling.

And beyond those, stretching on for what seemed like a city block, were globs and thickets of metal, odd-shaped baskets and geometric figures of dazzling complexity, all done in copper wire, or jagged black spokes.

Doremus lifted his light and discovered a gallery overhead, then a congeries of brightly painted metal pieces, all hanging on nearly invisible wires from the high rafters.

One of the mobile sculptures was moving, its cleaver parts trembling, brushing together.

He shifted the angle of his light and saw the hiding muddy boy at the top of the stairs to the gallery. The boy's eyes looked dark and glazed; they scarcely blinked as he turned his head and stared into the flashlight beam. He was breathing hard.

Doremus sighed. "OK; come down."

The boy leaped suddenly, away from the light. In his haste he brushed against a spindly column and a fierce white head fell to the gallery floor, rolled, plummeted toward Doremus. He stepped aside quickly, almost tripping, and grabbed a plaited plastic rope for support. Above his head a bell tolled, deeply, momentously.

"Then I'll come up," Doremus said, and he started up the flight of stairs, raking the gallery with his light. The bell tolled slowly, three times more. The boy backed away. Doremus kept the beam of the lamp low, not wanting to blind him.

"Time to quit running . . . Michael."

The boy ran anyway, darting among the groupings of statuary on the gallery floor. Doremus stalked him. Each time the boy paused for breath the light touched him, inspiring a new frenzy, a new leap. He was like a hounded animal, Doremus

172

thought, and despite the fact that this boy had tried to set him on fire, Doremus felt genuinely sorry for him.

"Easy now, I won't hurt you."

Sobbing, the boy crouched at the edge of the gallery floor, underneath the rail.

"Don't try it," Doremus warned, closing slowly. This bell tolled and the boy glanced fearfully at the barn floor, twenty feet below.

The bell tolled for the eleventh or twelfth time; the boy jerked suddenly, stared in astonishment at Doremus, teetered wildly, lost his balance and started to fall. But as he went over the edge, his windmilling hands seized the iron railing and he swung there precariously. Doremus dived, threw an arm around his waist and hauled him back to the gallery floor. The boy fought him furiously, escaped, stumbled and ran for the stairs. As Doremus got to his feet the lights in the barn flashed on. He limped toward the stairs. Two men had entered the barn. One of them was a burly, bald artist type with an improbable beard. The other man was Craig Young, who was holding the weeping unresisting boy in his arms and looking up at Doremus with an incredulous expression.

"Good, you got him," Doremus muttered, starting down.

"Peter?" Craig said to the boy. "Peter, what's the trouble, what are you doing here? How did you get here?"

"Do you know who he is?" Doremus said, scowling.

"Of course I know him. He's one of our boys. His name is Peter Mathis."

"I think he's the one who's been playing Michael

on the telephone . . . and there's no end to his versatility: he tried to kill me tonight."

"That's impossible," Craig said angrily.

"It is? Let *him* tell you."

"I don't know what he's doing this far from the school, but I know he hasn't been making any telephone calls. Not Peter."

"No! Why are you so sure?"

"Because Peter is mute," Craig said curtly, comforting the terrified boy.

13

Wearing a pair of paint-daubed dungarees and a clean if tattered shirt borrowed from the sculptor Brunell, Doremus sat in the office of the Greenleaf School's headmaster. He was barefoot, his shoes having been too dirty for the velvety blue carpet, and his neck was stiffening from the plunge into the millpond, but Enoch Mills had provided him with a good cigar and he felt as if he would get through the night without too much difficulty.

"Peter couldn't have left the grounds this afternoon without being missed," the headmaster insisted. His name was Quinlan and he had the vestigial crispness of an ex-military man, though his face was lapped and folded from age, and his lips trembled when he wasn't speaking.

"Saturday's a free day at the school, ain't it?" Enoch Mills asked. "A good many of the boys go into town."

"Usually, Sheriff. But we played a football game here this afternoon, so all but a handful of the boys stayed on the campus. The others were in the company of parents or relatives."

"And Peter was here all afternoon?" Doremus said.

"I'm quite sure of it. Dinner was served at five-thirty, less than twenty minutes after the game ended. If he hadn't been in his place for dinner I would have heard about it. Immediately after dinner a movie was shown in the cafeteria. The movie lasted nearly two hours. The boys then went to their residence halls. In Dobbs Hall, which is where Peter and the younger boys live, there is a bed check at eight-forty-five, and the lights go out at nine. In Franklin Hall the boys are allowed to stay up half an hour longer."

"Peter was in his bed at a quarter of nine then."

"I would have heard immediately if he wasn't."

"So he couldn't have slipped off the campus earlier, while the movie was being shown," Mills said. Quinlan shook his head. "But less than an hour later, according to Doremus, he was at the grist-mill on the Hawke farm, and that's five miles from here."

"Could one of Peter's roommates have doubled for him during the bed check?"

"We're familiar with that ruse," the headmaster said, smiling faintly. "Also Peter doesn't have a roommate."

"I'd like to have a look at the hall where he lives," Doremus said.

"Certainly. I'll take you there myself." The headmaster unlocked a drawer of his desk, took out a set of keys and accompanied Mills and Doremus across the misty quadrangle.

"Is there someone on the gate all night long?"

"Our watchman. Three or four times a night he patrols the grounds, but not at regular intervals."

Doremus looked at the rooftops of the Gothic-collegiate buildings. The dormitories which they were approaching appeared to be joined, at right angles, and each was four stories high. They were in turn joined to the building that housed the cafeteria and gymnasium by a covered archway. The school's parking lot was out of sight behind the cafeteria, but it could be reached only by means of the main gate and an unlighted asphalt drive that curved behind the quadrangle. Looming above the campus was the dark and heavily wooded Constable Ridge.

The bell in the tower of the administration building tolled twice as the headmaster unlocked the door of Dobbs Hall. The entrance was well lighted and clearly visible from the gatehouse. Inside there was a single bright light at each end of the corridor.

"How many keys are there?" Doremus asked, examining the solid oak door.

"Only three; I can tell you where each is right at this moment. And as you can see, the doors lock from the outside only."

They went up stairs to the top floor, where Peter Mathis lived. There was another, simpler lock on the door of the suite. Quinlan let them in with a passkey.

"Each suite contains two bedrooms and a study room," the headmaster whispered as they entered. "Let's see . . . I believe Peter has this room." They walked through a curtained doorway into a cubicle which contained two barracks-style beds and two dressers, nothing more. One bed was bare to the mattress. They other looked as if it had been slept in, at least briefly.

Doremus felt a draft on his stiff neck and went to the dormer windows. There were three of them, casement-type windows twenty-four inches wide. One window had been cranked open as far as it could go. The ledge outside was granite, about eight inches deep. He looked down at the quadrangle forty feet below. Some of the stones of the wall protruded evenly for an inch or so, but there were no secure handholds.

Doremus turned his head carefully to the right. The roof slanted outward, past the windows, and where it ended there was a metal rain trough that looked dependable. He put one foot on the ledge and tried to get through the window space, but, thin as he was, he couldn't make it. He stuck his head out as far as possible and surveyed the gray-and-red slate roof.

"Peter couldn't have gone out that way," the headmaster protested, "it's far too dangerous. All the boys know it. We lecture them every year on the dangers of trying to climb—"

"I'm sure most of them take the lectures to heart, but this boy is something else again. I believe he went out this way, and came back this way, not once but as many as a dozen times. Let's go down."

From the quadrangle Doremus located Peter's window.

"If he could negotiate the slate to the point where the roof flattens, then he could walk across the buildings without difficulty. I doubt that anyone would see him against the background of the ridge. The hard part would be the first twelve feet—or the last, if he's returning to his room.

With the rain trough to stand on and sneakers for grip he might make it easily to the flat of the roof. I wouldn't care to try it myself though. Let's find a way for him to climb down, now that we've got him up there."

They walked to the end of the second dormitory. Here Doremus saw a door in the otherwise blank wall, and a covered walkway to the cafeteria. Ivy grew thickly on the rugged facing of the wall.

"Reckon he clumb down that ivy?" Mills said, looking dubious.

"It's the only way off the dormitory roof. Not such a bad climb; the roof of the walkway there is a couple of floors high."

"Peter Mathis isn't a particularly strong or athletic youngster," Quinlan said, his voice thin and doleful. "What could have possessed him to do such a dangerous thing?"

Doremus looked thoughtfully at the headmaster. "Maybe Craig can help us here. Let's find out how the boy is."

Craig and Amy had come downstairs from the infirmary and were sitting on opposite ends of the couch in the headmaster's office.

"He's asleep now," Amy said as soon as the men came in. "It wasn't easy; the sedative we gave Peter should have knocked him out in a matter of minutes, but he was so horribly disturbed ..." Her voice was bleak. "He couldn't stop threshing in the bed, and moaning. I don't know when I've spent a worse half hour." Craig had no comment. He looked aghast, demoralized. He was trying to smoke a cigarette, but his hand shook so badly that the effort made him look almost comical, like a talentless actor miming a drunk.

"Will we be able to ask Peter some questions in the morning?" Enoch Mills said tentatively, and Craig said, flaring:

"Absolutely not!"

After a few seconds he apparently regretted his tone and looked up at them with a trace of apology. "Peter is badly in need of rest, and . . . and complete quiet. It might be necessary to keep him tranquilized for several days. You see, I don't have a clear idea of the trauma he's suffered, and I won't until I've had the opportunity to sit down with him and—"

Doremus said, "Could Peter Mathis be Michael, your brother?"

The psychologist winced as if he'd said something deliberately foolish. "What are you talking about?'

"Let me put that another way. Could he *think* he's your brother?"

"Good God, of course not!"

"Originally you believed that the boy who was telephoning Helen had convinced himself he was Michael Young."

"Yes, I thought that was a possibility. But Peter doesn't know anything about my brother! Oh, I'm sure during the past couple of weeks he's heard the gossip about 'Michael's ghost,' all that nonsense—I must be quite a figure of fun around here because of it. But Peter hasn't been doing any telephoning. I've told you that already."

"Yes, he's mute. But his problem is psychological, isn't it, and not physical."

"He stopped speaking when he was about four years old, because of extreme emotional problems, and he hasn't said a word since."

"Maybe he hasn't spoken," Doremus conceded.

"Yet, apparently, he's done some remarkable things for a nine-year-old boy." He explained the observations which he had made from Peter's room. Craig listened soberly, if incredulously, then got up and went to the windows that overlooked the lighted quadrangle and the residence halls. Amy followed him, and they stood side by side staring out. No one else in the room said anything.

When Craig turned around he looked baffled but frightened. "I don't believe it."

Enoch Mills glanced at Doremus, and his usually placid pale-green country-sage eyes were shadowed with annoyance. Doremus was keeping his thoughts to himself, and his own eyes on blond Amy, who still had her back to them all. Mills turned his Stetson hat around and around in his knobby hands and said, somewhat reluctantly, "Not believing it don't get us anywheres. What happened tonight fits right into a pattern. First Mrs. Connelly had all them telephone calls—didn't you listen in on one of them yourself?" Craig shook his head slowly. "But you were there, I believe. Well, anyway, she had them calls, from the same boy who said he was your brother, and after a while he started sounding kinda ugly. Then one afternoon he calls up Peggy Connelly and says something bad is going to happen to old Doc Britton and sure enough that same afternoon Doc's dead. No accident, neither, the whole thing looks arranged, and right after Elsa Britton finds her husband dead then she sees this boy too, hanging around the barn, and she swears it's Michael Young as she remembers him." Enoch cleared his throat urgently, as if he were not used to long speeches, and went on doggedly: "That patient of

181

yours, Peter Mathis, could pass for your brother any day, near as I can tell from that little school photograph taken of your brother back then."

"I don't think they look alike at all."

"Well, you got to consider the shape of their faces and the set of their eyes; other features and hair color don't mean that much. Let me get through with this. Peggy Connelly claims that she saw this boy twice, and I'm inclined to take her word even if she is a child. Once she saw him about dark on The Shades School playground, and that's just the other side of the hogback out there, maybe a couple of miles at the most." He turned his attention to the headmaster. "Did this Mathis boy ever stray off the campus that you know of?"

"Yes, I recall that he did. When he first arrived last year he left school several times without permission. But that was during the day. As you're already aware, Sheriff, we have this sort of problem because though the majority of our children are rebellious and extremely insecure, we try to avoid any suggestion of the reformatory here. Nearly all of our wanderers come back of their own accord." Quinlan shot a look at Craig, who confirmed this with a nod. "Peter always returned. It was never a question of going out to search for him."

"That would account for Peggy having seen him on the playground, but the other time she got a close look it was late, past midnight, and she and her mama were maybe eight miles from here."

"I know," Craig said wearily. "I was there."

"But you didn't see nothing of the boy yourself?"

"I stayed for ten or fifteen minutes after Helen left, looking around with my flashlight. I didn't

182

see anything. I'm fairly sure Peggy was dreaming."

"Could be," Mills grunted. "I wasn't dreaming the night that boy called up the station and asked for Hap. Can't prove he had any part in what happened up there on the river—"

"And nobody's proved Peter has made any telephone calls," Craig said angrily. "I've told you several times he's emotionally incapable of speech, but I don't seem to have made an impression: you're hell bent on connecting him with two violent deaths. That's irresponsible. He's a confused, unhappy *nine-year-old* boy!"

"Craig," Amy said, so softly they barely heard her.

Craig's shoulders slumped. "I don't want to listen to any more of this," he muttered. "I have a responsibility toward Peter, and I should be with him right now."

"I'm just trying to get a few things straight in my mind," Enoch said heavily, "and I don't think I called him a murderer. But we know where he was tonight, and what he tried to do. My boss found a burned-out torch and an empty two-gallon can of gasoline in the brush next to that gristmill. If he didn't make the call to Doremus, then it looks like there's two boys involved. Hell, maybe there's a slew of 'em."

Doremus said, "Has Peter's behavior been noticeably violent in the past?"

"He's had spells of anger since I've known him," Craig said eagerly. "In fact, I've encouraged them. And he's had a couple of minor scuffles with other boys, but they were due to normal aggressiveness; they weren't characterized by unusual violence. That's why I don't understand this attack on you."

"Tell me about Peter. Where's he from?"

"St. Louis. His childhood has been ... totally grim. His mother was a spoiled and hateful young woman. At seventeen she became pregnant, refused to marry her lover and settled down in her parents' home to wait for the birth of the baby. The girl apparently was having her revenge on unloved parents, and if you met them you'd know why they were unloved. They're old, rich, prominent, and as heartless a pair as I've ever seen. I don't know if it's to their credit that they refused to be intimidated by their daughter's action. They simply retired to their mansion, seeing no one. Even today they seldom appear in public. So Peter was born, and grew up in an atmosphere of scathing hatred. One thing in the mother's favor: apparently she was fond of Peter, she looked after him herself. But she burned to death smoking in her bed when Peter was three and he was left on his own, totally vulnerable. I've already said he stopped speaking at the age of four, which may give you an idea of what he suffered at the hands of those people." Unexpectedly Craig's eyes filled with tears but he went on, his voice even. "If he didn't have a strong will he'd probably be in a mental institution today. As it is, I think we're making progress with him; through hypnosis I've come very close to removing the block that keeps him mute. After tonight I suppose I'll have to start all over." He dried his eyes on the back of his hand and stood with his head bowed, staring down at the carpet. Outside, the bell tolled three times and Doremus cocked his head, listening.

"For what it's worth, I don't think Peter attacked me tonight," Doremus said. He raised his hand and gingerly touched the small bump on the back of his skull, near the right ear. "Someone else was in that mill with him." The Sheriff started to speak but Doremus cut him off. "I didn't see anyone else, Enoch, this is pure hunch. But I stand six-three and it's not likely Peter could have given me this whack on the head while he was on the run. And he was on the run all the time I was there, it was a game to him. I didn't hear him speak but I heard him giggling from excitement."

They were all looking at him now, except for Amy, who seemed to have turned to stone in front of the windows. "Peter was playing games tonight. He didn't go to the mill to kill me or anybody else. Even when he was stalking me with that lighted torch there was something odd about the way he acted. I believe he was only trying to hand me the torch, because that's what he'd been told to do. He was puzzled because I didn't want it." Doremus fell silent awhile, then he said sharply, "Does that make sense to you, Amy?"

She wasn't startled, but he turned and looked his way rather vaguely before replying. "Yes," she said then, her voice pitched low, "I'm beginning to see what all this means." Her eyes strayed momentarily to the window. "After all, he has been leaving here, sometimes late at night, we're sure of that, so something—someone is making him take such terrible chances. So it has to be. Peter is possessed. There is no other explanation." She looked defiantly at Craig, at the befuddled headmaster. "No other," Amy repeated, and her voice was brittle, her eyes wide and frightened. "Michael Young has control of him. He's making Peter do these awful things."

Craig made a sickened noise in his throat, and Quinlan continued to regard her as if she were raving. Craig said, desperately, "Amy, don't get started—"

"*You* don't believe in demonic possession, but the phenomenon is real, volumes have been written on the subject! I have some of them in my office. You told me not long ago that something evil was loose in The Shades, you said that you felt the presence of evil! I'm not claiming it's the spirit of Michael Young. But Michael could easily be living, as Doremus suggested. Don't you agree, Craig? You believed it a few nights ago. All right, why not assume that Michael didn't die, that he grew up and came back here—he's living here and he's murdering people. We don't know who he is . . . but Peter knows him!"

"What?" Craig said weakly.

"Yes, Peter knows him," Amy insisted. "He's met with Michael many times, out there, in the woods, and they're friends. Michael has told Peter all about himself, all about the Youngs, he's told him many times about the terrible death of his mother, and of course Peter is sympathetic—his own mother was hated and hounded and she died in a tragic mysterious accident. You see, they have a lot in common. And Michael has been cunning enough to use Peter to his own advantage. He can talk Peter into doing anything, taking any sort of risk, in the name of—" Amy broke off. "Helen!" she said, as if her throat were raw.

"She's all right. I've had a deputy parked in front of her house since eleven o'clock," Enoch Mills assured her. He licked dry lips and clamped his Stetson on his head. "Well," he said, turning to Doremus, "I guess she makes better sense than anything else I've heard tonight. Maybe that boy will be a help to us yet—when we can get in to see him," he finished, with a significant look at Craig, who ignored him. "Meantime . . . where's that infirmary at?"

"Second floor of this building," the headmaster replied.

"This here's Sunday already," Enoch mused. "How long do you figure that boy will sleep?"

"As long as fifteen hours, if he's not disturbed," Craig said.

"Reckon I ought to put a deputy up there, to make sure he ain't disturbed. Or maybe we ought to move him to the hospital. We're dealing with a killer, after all, and he may try to get at that boy."

Amy blanched. Craig said, "There are three other boys in another part of the infirmary, and a nurse is on duty around the clock. I think Peter is perfectly safe where he is . . . but I intend to stay with him myself, until he wakes up. Longer if need be."

"The sooner we find out where his friend is, the better."

"I realize that." Craig looked at Amy for a long moment. "I hope we have the answers now; I hope this will be over with quickly now." He looked anxious, unconvinced. "Why hasn't Mi—Michael come to me? We were friends. . . . Does he mean to kill me too? How could he have become so twisted?" Amy put a hand on his shoulder, but he didn't seem to notice the hand, or her. "I'd almost rather believe in a ghost—or that Peter could sprout wings and fly." He started to laugh, but it became a coughing fit; his eyes looked dry, as if fever were beginning. "Crazy," Craig muttered. "It's crazy, incredible. . . . the only thing very real to me is that boy, that helpless boy." Amy flinched slightly, but only Doremus saw it. She withdrew her hand.

"I'd like to stay tonight too," she said softly.

"What? Oh, no, no need for that. Get yourself some sleep, Amy. I'll call you if . . ." He wandered away from her, looked once at Enoch Mills and once at Doremus, distantly, then went out the door. They heard his quick footsteps in the hall, heard him racing up the stairs three at a time.

Enoch Mills yawned, then pulled the Colt Woodsman from beneath his twill jacket and handed it to Doremus. "Almost forgot . . . the boys found this near the empty gas can. You got off three shots, huh?"

"Just to make noise. I wasn't aiming at anything."

Mills shook his head in a troubled way. "Maybe we can get together tomorrow, chew this thing over? Can I give you a lift to the village now?" Doremus declined and Mills left, murmuring good nights. The headmaster had begun to shuffle around in his bedroom slippers, turning off lights. Amy looked abandoned.

Doremus said pleasantly, "I'm interested in those books you have on demonology. I might borrow one, if you don't mind."

"Not at all." The three of them left the headmaster's office. Quinlan lived just down the hill; when summoned by Craig he had come wearing layers of sweaters over his pajamas, and a heavy topcoat. He said:

"I suppose I should notify Peter's grandparents about this; it's the only ethical thing to do. But I wouldn't know how to begin an explanation. I just wouldn't know."

"Peter will be all right now," Amy said soothingly. "I'm sure of it."

"He's been badly used ... badly used. And it happened right under our noses. But I think we do our best for our boys ... we try our best."

"Yes, sir."

"You'll see that Mr. Ketchum locks up after you, Miss Lawlor?" The old man went out by the front door and began walking dispiritedly toward the drive where he'd left his car.

Amy said: "He's a lovely man, but ... just a little old for this sort of work. I'm sorry for him. He's sincerely interested in each of the boys." They continued slowly down the hall to the corner office that was Amy's. She pointed to her bookshelf and sank down on a wheezing leather sofa, gloomy and uncommunicative.

Doremus politely read a few titles and then said, "On second thought, I probably don't have much time to read. Could I bum a ride?"

Amy gave him an annoyed look, then softened. "I'd appreciate the company," she admitted.

14

She drove a good used Mustang and drove it well, rubbing her eyes and shrugging her shoulders from time to time to keep alert. Doremus slouched in the seat next to her and wished for a cigar. He said, "If it wouldn't be too much trouble I'd like to recover my motor scooter. Left it in some bushes down near the gristmill."

"No trouble," Amy said a trifle grimly. "That's Millican Dairy Road, isn't it?"

"Right." They passed through the deserted village. There were only traces of the early mist, and the moon shone high and yellow. "You've been going with Craig for quite a while, haven't you?" Doremus asked.

"Since I came here—eighteen months ago. I was fresh out of USC graduate school."

"California girl?"

"Born and bred. West Covina, in the days when

190

there were still a few orange groves out that way."

"Helen says you gave pictures a try."

"It's the only thing you want to do when you're sixteen. I was . . . full-grown—maybe full-blown is the expression—and lucky. A few bit parts right away, the second lead in a terrible horror epic we shot by the light of borrowed flashlights, then a small continuing role in a syndicated series that bombed out after thirteen weeks. Real fringe stuff, but I was dizzy with success. I even managed to get a good agent—he could pick up the phone and get right through to Richard Brooks or somebody like that. I took acting lessons and made the scene with a lot of gorgeous young guys who were already dead inside at twenty-one, and after a couple of years of it I saw where I was headed and had the sense to get out."

"You made a good choice."

"A perfect choice. I love what I'm doing now."

"You and Craig will be getting married before long, I imagine."

She was quiet for three heartbeats. "Yes. Before long."

They drove down Millican Dairy Road, raising dust, and Amy slowed when the bridge over the creek came into her headlights.

"I meant to ask Craig if he saw anything when he came down this road tonight," Doremus said. "Slipped my mind."

"That was after all the excitement. Besides, he might have driven over by way of 22. Brunell's place is closer if you cut off the state road." They rattled across the loosely planked bridge. "Where do you want me to stop?"

"Anywhere beyond the bridge. Good thing Craig

showed up when he did; we would have had a great deal of trouble getting Peter back to the school."

"Well, Craig has his eye on a gorgeous bronze nude about so high that Brunell got in two or three weeks ago. He's practically been living over at the gallery, trying to get Abe to come down on it a hundred or so." She turned off the engine. "I guess it would be better to put your scooter in the trunk rather than in the back seat. We can tie the lid down if need be."

They got out and Doremus, guided by the headlights of the Mustang, found the brush in which he had hidden his scooter, wheeled it out. Amy opened the trunk for him and he lifted the scooter inside, then wired the trunk lid to the back bumper. Amy was standing by the side of the road looking at the rise of the gristmill a hundred feet away. The surface of the water beside the wheel glistened in the moonlight, and Doremus could see where he had crashed through the thin dry boards covering an upstairs window.

Amy shuddered. "Spooky place. You had a lot of courage just to walk in, not knowing—"

"As long as we're here I think I'd like to have another look around," Doremus said, and he skidded down the slope to the water's edge, carrying the light he'd borrowed from the Hawkes.

"Leave me here?" Amy said, startled.

Doremus turned and grinned at her. "Come on then. I'd appreciate the company."

Amy was wearing a ribbed pink turtleneck sweater, dark-green ski pants and black boots, so their trek between the thick brush on the slope and the flowing water was no hardship for her. Directly below the gristmill Doremus extended a hand and hauled her up the slippery bank. They stood close together in the moonlight, in silence, studying the entrance. The dirt of the clearing was completely tracked up.

"Where did you fall?" Amy asked, as he showed her. "That far? You might have been killed."

"I started thinking about that an hour ago. My stomach suddenly felt full of ice-cold toads. It was shock, I suppose."

Amy bit her lip. "I'd like to go. I'm awfully tired and—"

"Five minutes more." They walked back to the mill entrance. "I wonder why it had to be gasoline," Doremus mused. "What goes on in his mind? He could have just waited by the door and blown my head off with a shotgun when I came in. And why go to all the trouble to drag Peter out here . . . why make him a part of it?"

"After you fell into the pond they ran, didn't they? Both of them. He—Michael—must have thought you were dead."

"I suppose so." They approached the brush and the woods in front of the mill. "They ran this way, toward the road, and he got rid of the torch and the gas can, and this pistol—apparently he picked it up inside after I dropped it. They were making for the road, but one of the Hawke boys was between them and the road, and Willis had a light. Instead of keeping low and quiet until there was no further danger of being observed, Peter must have become frightened, and so he bolted into the open, into the meadow there. And Willis Hawke caught a glimpse of him as he ran. Apparently Willis never saw Michael at all. Michael, when he could move without being detected, continued on through the woods until he reached the road. Where he'd left his car."

Amy looked at Doremus, her eyes dark caves in the moonlight.

"He drives a car, of course; it's the only way he could get Peter back and forth. So his car was hidden somewhere off the road. Peter, meanwhile, was on the loose. What would you do, if you were Michael?"

"I'd . . . wait for him. Near the car."

"And then if Peter didn't make it back you'd have to go looking for him. Since you'd last seen him on the meadow you'd have to search there, but you couldn't risk being seen yourself. So you'd return to the woods, you'd go to the edge of the meadow and start walking, until you crossed the marsh and reached the Brunell place."

Amy nodded tautly. "Yes."

"And they you'd see Peter, up there on the hill, near the barn, the Brunell Gallery, and know you couldn't take the chance of calling him. You'd have to go and get him, lead him back to the car, then clear out." He walked with Amy to the moon-lighted meadow, which was lightly frosted now. They left footprints in the stiffened grass.

"But that's where I went, searching for Peter," Doremus said. "To the Brunell place. Peter must have seen me coming, and . . . Michael undoubtedly saw me too, from the woods. He saw me and realized there was nothing he could do, realized he couldn't get to Peter before I did. So he returned through the woods to the place where he'd put his car. It must have been up the road a-ways, where the sound of an engine turning over would be muffled. And then he—"

"He drove away," Amy finished, too quickly.

Doremus turned off the light and faced her, and they stood ankle deep in the soft glowing meadow, his breath mildly steaming. Amy seemed to have stopped breathing, but her body was racked, she trembled from the cold and something more; there were tear tracks on her cheeks, like poured silver.

"I don't think so," Doremus said. "He drove only as far as the Brunell place. And it wasn't anybody named Michael."

"God," Amy's voice broke. "God, God, no, don't, stop, you hear, Doremus? I won't listen!"

"That was a good summation you made at the school, Amy. You put together what we knew, and what we suspected, and what we hoped was true, you put it all together beautifully and it sounded good. But it wasn't the whole truth, because the truth is even more frightening, more grotesque. We have to let it out though, Amy. We have to let the truth breathe."

"No, no, it couldn't be!"

"There's no Michael Young living in The Shades now, plotting and killing in memory of his dear mother. Michael Young *did* die in that blizzard, and his ghost rests. There is no Michael Young. He does not live. Despite all of Craig's sick efforts to bring him back to life in the person of Peter Mathis."

He was prepared for almost any reaction but violence. Amy launched herself at him, fists flailing, landing blows on his forehead, shoulders, chest. She hadn't the breath for screaming, but the sounds in her throat were worse than screaming. Doremus tried to tie up her arms and she butted him under the chin with her head, knocking him down. She came stomping with her boots, like a man, breath rasping, the odd squealing noise rising and falling in her throat like the notes of an idiot's whistle. He decided she had to be fought as a man even as he was rolling out from under her boots. He blocked a kick at his throat, grabbed an ankle, twisted hard. Amy fell heavily but the crusty deep meadow grass softened the fall. She sat up determinedly, legs threshing, one clawlike hand raking toward his face. He pushed the hand aside and slapped her roughly. Amy's head whipped around and there was a startled gleam in one black eye, but her mouth was set in a savage line. Doremus belted her again and she dropped both arms and her head sank, blond hair spilling over the front of her sweater.

A cry of agony burst from Amy's throat. Her chest heaved. Even as he stood over her, ready to hit her again, Doremus could not help feeling a twinge of lust. He was grimly amused: it had been many months since he'd felt any sort of sexual desire at all. Then tenderness swept over him, and pity. He reached down, grasped an elbow, sought to lift her to her feet. She came halfway, eyes closed. Her throat muscles worked convulsively. Doremus let go and she turned around and threw up with as much violence as she had put into assaulting him.

He left Amy there and went down by the mill-race, tore the shirt the sculptor had given him and returned to the meadow, where Amy now lay stretched out on her face. He kneeled beside her, turned her over, wiped her puffed face with the wet piece of shirt. She flinched and tried to pull away.

"I want to die," she groaned.

Doremus studied her face intently, and the things he had noticed all along about this girl suddenly hit him with a curious impact: the high lift of cheekbones, elegant and roguish curve of nose, firm chin, unusual length and thickness of eyelashes. Goddam pity, he observed, holding her, wondering how much she'd loved Craig. She'd made a good try at protecting him, even though the truth must have been eating her insides at the time. He'd had a few things to go on, Doremus thought, but how had Amy known so quickly, how had she been sure? Intuition? *Lovely*, he thought, with a lingering sadness. *All the looks in the world and brainy too, and now how am I supposed to get you through the next few minutes?*

He took a deep breath and stood. She lay boneless in the crushed meadow, weakly gasping. He bent over and flicked the wet cloth across her face, stinging her.

"Get up," he said. "I'm not going to carry you. You're big enough to walk." When Amy didn't obey immediately he hit her again with the lash of the cloth. Her eyes popped open. She glared up at him. Even by moonlight he could see the reddening cheek, the thin welt. She put a hand to her injured cheek.

"You didn't have to do that!"

"On your feet."

Amy sat up, then with an effort made it to her feet. Doremus looked dispassionately at her. She said, in a voice thick with anger, "I think you're the most loathsome man I've met in my life. I mean it. I didn't like you from the first day I met you. You're arrogant and cold and boorish. I just wanted you to know that." She walked off briskly, down the slope of the meadow to the clearing in front of the mill. There she stopped, uncertainly, touched her cheek again, and began sobbing, swaying on her feet. She cried like an abused and misunderstood child.

He went down there and took her by the elbow and guided her slowly and tenderly along the creek, to the car, and she cried all the way. When they were inside the car she threw her arms around him and held him tightly, and buried her frozen face in the lambskin lining of Willis Hawke's new jacket. Doremus let her go until there were no more tears, just excruciating dry sobs. The sky in the east seemed to be graying. It had been a long night. He felt incredibly tired, sitting there, and his head ached. And he knew it was still a long, long way from being over.

"He must be . . . so terribly sick. I don't know why . . . I didn't see it sooner. All these months. So evasive, so preoccupied. How long was he carrying all that around in his mind? Oh, God, God, God, *what* can I do, how can I help him?"

"It's important to remember this, Amy. He is sick. And he's extremely dangerous. He's more dangerous at this moment than he's ever been, because he must realize we're getting close to him."

She pulled away, saying, in a horrified tone, "Peter!"

"Peter's safe with Craig; in fact Peter may be the only one who's safe with him just now."

"What about all he's made Peter go through in the past few weeks? Climbing over the roofs of the school . . . he could have been killed at any time. What has Peter had to do with Andy's death, and Hap's? Doremus, there's so much I don't understand!"

"I suppose the whole thing began with Peter, because he does strongly resemble Michael Young, and he's about the same age Michael was when he wandered off into that storm. And temperamentally, as far as I know, Peter is very much like Michael. So there was Craig, the clinical psychologist, trying to help Peter, trying to get behind the wall of anger and hurt and hostility that kept Peter mute, becoming more and more involved with him, with his problems, with the mother who had died. Maybe that was what ultimately got to Craig—the trauma of the mother who was torn away, suddenly made dead."

"Why?" Amy cried.

"We've heard time and again how much Michael loved his mother. We've heard how he rebelled against everybody when she died, retreated into himself, tried over and over to escape, to run away. But what do we know about Craig's reactions? How did he take his mother's death? Was he unaffected? I doubt it. I think he was as hurt and angered and resentful as his brother; but, emotionally, they weren't alike. Craig seems to have been the kind to button his lip, keep things to himself, never, never show his emotions. Besides, he had an extra burden, his little brother. He must have felt responsible for Mike because they were alone, in the care of an aunt whom they didn't know, whom they undoubtedly disliked and mistrusted at first. It was the world against the Youngs, and Craig felt bound to protect Michael at all costs. You can imagine how Michael's death hit him—when he failed in his trust."

Amy was sitting up now, her face stiff, listening. She moistened her lips with her tongue. "He must have felt . . . guilty. Intensely, morbidly guilty."

"I would say so. And as he grew older the pressure of that guilt became too intense for him; it had to produce a few cracks in the psyche, give reality some odd twists. He had to be suffering. What happens to the individual who lives so long with guilt, keeping his emotions properly under control all the time?"

Amy was silent for a while, and then she said haltingly, "He can . . . destroy himself. Or he can shift the burden, make others carry part of it for him."

"Others, like Helen Connelly. Or Andrew Britton. Hap Washbrook."

"Doremus . . . what made you suspect it had to be Craig?"

"I began speculating when I saw how dependent on Craig Peter was. Also, an interesting thing happened in the barn while I was trying to corner Peter. I inadvertently started a bell tolling, and after it tolled ten, maybe a dozen times, Peter nearly jumped out of his skin, like a . . . a sleepwalker waking, and he seemed to have no awareness of where he was. The shock almost caused him a bad fall. Later, when I heard the bell at the Greenleaf School, which has a similar tone, it occurred to me that Peter might have been under hypnosis all the time I was chasing him—that he'd been cued to wake up, in his own room, at a certain hour, by the tollings of the school bell. By 'wake up' I mean from induced sleep. Then Craig mentioned he'd been using hypnosis as a part of Peter's therapy. I had already come up with the idea that Peter was getting out of his room at night by leaping like a tender young mountain goat over the rooftops of the school, and then I knew how it could be possible. He was doing it under deep hypnosis. Craig had been controlling almost every move Peter made until Peter blundered away from him tonight."

"Something like that occurred to me. If Peter was leaving the school at will, then someone had to be helping him. Someone who could drive in and out of the school grounds at all hours, without being challenged or remembered: a familiar face. When I made myself accept that I knew it all, because ..." she hesitated, weakening, and leaned toward him again; Doremus held her, lightly, the crown of her head tucked under his chin. "Upstairs in the infirmary, while Peter was in a frenzy, Craig almost broke down. No. He did break down. I was in the outer room, the dispensary, trying to locate an ampul of meprobamate. The nurse is an old girl who can't see a foot without her glasses and Peter was upsetting her. Anyway, when I found the ampul I let her prepare the injection and went back to Craig. He was sitting on the bed holding Peter tightly in his arms and at first I thought there must be another boy with them, in the shadows somewhere, because I heard this voice saying, 'Don't, Michael ... you're not lost, you're not lost ...' This ... little boy's voice. But the whole room was empty, only the three of us were there. It was Craig. And that voice ... I'd heard it before. Just the other morning, on the telephone. Craig hadn't been gone from my bed thirty minutes when ... *that* voice, that same voice. Said he was Michael. Said he hated Craig." She tensed in his arms; Doremus held her tighter. "Oh, God," she whimpered. "I'm so scared!"

"What happened after you heard him talking to Peter, calling him Michael?"

"He became aware of me, he saw my shadow or something, and turned around and said in his own voice, 'What's taking her so damned long?' Then the nurse hurried in and we gave Peter the tranquilizer, quite a lot of it, and I retreated. I wasn't going to think about it, what I heard, I *wasn't*. I willed myself not to. It was like being sliced deep with a very sharp knife. The blood comes a little later. I'm sorry I hit you, Doremus. It was my last chance, my very last chance to keep from drowning in my blood." One of her hands was limp against his leg. He felt her breath on his throat, and he smiled unconsciously, comfortingly.

"But why is he using Peter like that? Why does he insist Peter is Michael? He knows better. Doesn't he? How can he know it one minute, and . . . not the next?"

"You've seen him go from an irrational to a rational state of mind in the blink of an eye. I don't know why it happens either, but . . . look at it this way: he's a man balancing a massive stone on his head, struggling down a long straight road. One instant that road is black as night and filled with terrible things, and two steps later the sun is beating down on the road, on him. Maybe he thinks about it, out there in the sun, maybe he remembers the terrors. He would like to stop and think it all over carefully, but he knows he can't stop, even for a moment, because the weight he is carrying will surely crush him if he does. I've met many psychotics in my former profession, I've talked to psychiatrists about them. They reach a desperation point, where any mild stimulus can drive them into the dark forever, where the nightmares never stop. You know that, Amy, it's your line of work. It isn't a pleasant thing to think about, because legally there's no way to touch Craig, not a shred of evidence against him. He should be locked up. But we can't do it."

"What are we going to do, then? We have to get Peter away from Craig."

"As I said before, I believe Peter's safe for now, since Craig's psychosis largely depends on him. No telling what damage Craig has done to Peter, psychologically speaking. Maybe a good psychiatrist will be able to straighten Peter out once this is over."

"But what are we going to *do*?" Amy said urgently.

"Talk some more, Amy. At your place, I hope. I should make a telephone call right away. Then . . . I'm going to need your help, a lot of help. It's necessary to prove without doubt that Craig is insane and capable of murder. That won't be easy, and we probably don't have very much time."

15

Helen woke up at seven thirty, earlier than Peggy for once. Her daughter slept beside her, on her stomach, small hands clutching the plump pillow. She didn't come so often anymore, stumbling from her own room in the dark, burrowing soundlessly under the warm covers of Helen's bed, but it always gave Helen a glow of pleasure—as well as a taste of sadness—to wake up and find Peg there. She was growing fast, too fast, Helen thought, rearranging the bedding so Peg would keep warm.

It was a clear still cold morning. There was frost on the layer of yellow and ocher leaves in the backyard. Helen put on the best robe she had, the one that was pure extravagance, with yards of lace at the cuffs and down the front. She went downstairs, and was surprised to see the door of the office standing wide. She missed the morning effluvium of stale cigar smoke. She looked in. Apparently Doremus had come and gone, with all his belongings. The blankets and the pillow he had used were in the middle of the rusty-looking horsehair sofa. On top there was a scrawled note, the pale yellow rectangle of a telegram. She picked up the note.

Helen:
As you can see from the telegram I have to go up to Platteville for a while. Swen and his wife practically raised me, it's all I can do. I'll catch the seven a.m. bus to Ft. Wood, from there I can fly to St. Louis and on to Dubuque, then drive the rest of the way. With luck I'll be back late tomorrow night. We had some excitement last night; Sheriff Mills will tell you about it if you give him a call. Don't worry.

Doremus

Helen shook her head at the cryptic *Don't worry*. She read the note again, and glanced at the telegram. UNCLE SWEN SERIOUSLY ILL CAN YOU COME LOVE MEDA. She frowned and went out into the foyer, wondering if it was too early to call Enoch Mills. Then she decided she didn't care what time it was, and hastily dialed his home number.

The sun falling directly on the east window of her cubbyhole bedroom was like a candle flame held close to Amy's cheek. She stirred, coughed, awakened. Her eyes burned; she was not sure where she was until she saw the familiar flowered design of the spread piled up on the floor. She rolled over, her stomach lurching along a second later, falling into place like a stone. She had slept

in soiled clothes, with a dirty face. She ached in a
dozen vital places.

Amy staggered up and regarded herself in the
sunlit vanity mirror. Her face was a patchy red,
one cheek deeply creased by the ribbed sweater
she wore. *Sunday,* she thought. *I look like I've
been drunk. Played the part once. No good at it.*

It came to her then what was wrong with this
bright Sunday morning, what was so odd and forbidding about it. Until a few hours ago her life
had had solidity, continuity. Thank the sensible
and loving parents for a good start. But she'd done
all right on her own too—avoided the environmen-
tal traps that had already turned many women her
age into coarse shrill images of the almighty teen-
ager. She'd taken bumps and lumps without
whimpering and made good choices and seen the
path to the best possible life open up; she knew
where she was going. She had felt a little smug
about it. Setbacks, sure, but despite them it didn't
seem to be tough. Keep your sense of values.
Know who you are. Rejoice in a pinch of luck now
and then. The path is well marked.

The path is cunningly mined, and it makes no
difference who you are. The innocent and well-
meaning get blown to bits right along with the
wicked and amoral.

Amy saw her mouth sag, fought the growing
pressure of tears. She turned away quickly and
stood, knees pressed together, in the middle of her
sunny bedroom, toes in, trembling. She had lost
all sense of direction; she cowered at the thought
of the world waiting, as it waited every morning,
to be approached with confidence, or to be feared.
A large part of her confidence had been Craig. She
had loved him, fought with him, cherished him,

slept with him. How simple if he were dead, she thought. Then I could really mourn him, with honesty and a saddened heart. It would be easy to mourn, and gradually forget, and go on.

But he is not dead.

Amy had to look everywhere in the tiny house, explore every possible hiding place. And then she had to search the yard as well, from behind half-closed blinds. Birds sang carelessly in the Indian-summer sun and leaves blew across the deserted road, rattled against the milk bottles on her porch. Church bells rang in the distance. The fearful searching gradually sickened her.

I'm not afraid of him, she told herself. *Yesterday I loved him—I know I loved him.* She tried, but could feel no sense of love, which shamed her. *I'm a psychologist, I understand these things. I can help him. Can't I help him?*

Amy knew what she must do, and she knew it was getting dangerously late.

In her bedroom she stripped herself, located bruises, walked dispiritedly into the shower. The hot, almost smoking water was soothing to sore flesh. Head back, she soaped her throat and breasts, and her hands aroused explicit memories of the two of them together in the shower, fiercely passionate even after a night of lovemaking, slippery as otters but trying to couple. He had been so wonderfully passionate at first, but that had faded away, faded away. . . . How many times had they made love in the past few months? Why hadn't he wanted her?

Wearily Amy turned off the shower and got out, drying the inflamed corrupted body. From the neck up she felt quite dead. What if we had married? she thought. There was a gashing pain in her stomach.

Amy dressed, too slowly, in snug wool hip huggers, a very expensive pale-blue shirt with button-down collar and French cuffs. She took a bright-pink sweater from the closet but laid it out, folded, on the bed. She put on a headband and sunglasses, swallowed two aspirins and stood looking at herself in the vanity mirror while she wound her watch. Pale lips, pale cheeks, a look of vacancy. There was a raw spot on the side of her tongue: she had made it raw gritting her teeth against the chills that kept coming in waves. . . . I will go there, and I will see him, and he will smile at me and touch me reassuringly and say, You dreamed it all. Amy, it was a dream. Just look at me. There's nothing wrong with me, Amy.

She wondered if it would help to scream.

Football games were in progress on the playing field, boys were loafing along the road in front of the school wall. A few of them waved as Amy went by in her Mustang. She was scarcely aware of them at all.

Because it was Sunday she parked in the drive just behind the administration building. Craig's Chevelle was in front of her, forty feet away. She stared at it, looked away, stubbed out the cigarette she'd been smoking in the ashtray. She walked around the building to the shadowy wide steps and let herself in. As far as she could tell, the lower floor was deserted, filled with an amber light. She went first to her own office, making no noise. Inside she searched in her desk for the key to Craig's office, which he had given her long ago.

She was hoping she wouldn't find it, but it was there with the rubber bands and the paper clips.

Craig's office was almost the length of the hall away. Amy knocked softly on the walnut-inlaid door and waited numbly, breathing through her mouth. She knocked again to make sure he wasn't there. Then she slipped the key into the lock, turned it, let herself in.

The office was quite dark. Amy stood with her back to the door until her eyes became adjusted, then made her way across the carpet to the windows. She tilted the blinds slightly, letting in just enough light to help her find some tangible evidence that he was insane; proof that Peter Mathis and Michael Young had become terrifyingly confused in Craig's mind. Doremus had doubted that she would find such proof, but it had been Amy's idea, she had to try. If Craig remained free, what would he do next?

Amy went through the desk drawers first, finding them cluttered with tabbed folders, files of letters. It was slow work; she studied every note in Craig's hand for mention of Peter. At first she looked often at her wristwatch, worried about the minutes ticking away. She had no idea where Craig was. He could be upstairs in the infirmary close to Peter, perhaps sleeping in the next bed. Or he might be approaching his office right now. She glanced up, bit her lip sharply, went back to work.

The desk drawers yielded nothing. Amy looked at the filing cabinets, sighed. She had tried to straighten out Craig's files one afternoon but had given up in despair. He favored clutter and that was that, but he did know just where everything was. Inspired by anxiety, Amy combed the draw-

ers swiftly but found no folder with Peter Mathis'
name on it. She closed the top three drawers and
stood back, hands at her sides, blood pounding
like a cataract in her temples. What, then, had he
done with it? Was it possible that Craig had never
transcribed his notes on Peter?

The bottom drawer of the file contained a dozen
boxes of tape for the compact Wollensak recorder
on Craig's desk. Amy hunkered down, searched
through the boxes. None were labeled. She considered taking them all, listening to them in the privacy of her own office. But she realized that would
take hours, and if he returned to his office and
happened to miss the tapes . . .

Amy stood and pushed the drawer in with the
toe of one shoe, feeling defeated. Vacantly she
gazed at the tape recorder. Apparently Craig had
been using it recently. Amy considered the half-
used spool of tape. Then, impulsively, she punched
the proper buttons, rewound the tape, adjusted
the tuning disc to a whisper and started the machine again. The tape unwound smoothly and silently. Amy looked at her watch again: a minute
and a half had passed. There was nothing on the
tape.

*"I'll kill you sheriff I'll kill you I'll kill you I'll
shoot you right in the goddam guts if you don't
leave my mother alone—"*

Amy stiffened, felt her heart contract painfully
as the childish vituperation poured from the
speaker.

*"You're going to leave her alone you better not
touch her you're going to learn to keep your damn
hands off her You're going to stop f—"*

Unthinkingly Amy reached down and turned the
machine off with a stab of her finger. The skin of

her face felt icy. She was torn between listening to all of it and running, running until she was out in the cool autumn afternoon, in the bright sun. She looked away, through the tilted-down blinds. There were a few boys in the quadrangle, moving slowly, gesturing. Tears came to her eyes.

She saw Craig then, on the walk in front of the cafeteria. Peter was with him, a step behind, looking serious and frail. Craig was smoking his pipe. They were walking toward the administration building. As she watched, Craig turned and said something to Peter. He seemed to smile. Shocked, Amy took a step back, although there was no chance that he could see her even if he happened to look directly at his windows. She could not help thinking how ordinary the scene was, Craig strolling on the Sunday campus with one of the boys. He was a favorite of a good many of them; she had seen him many times from her own windows, and felt a burst of pride.

The scathing, ten-year-old voice she had heard as the metallic brown tape unwound intruded on this memory. Amy moved quickly and soundlessly across the carpet, let herself out, remembered to lock the door behind her. She fled down the hall, entered her own office, threw herself down on the whooshing couch. She lay there for five minutes, for ten, motionless, hands over her face.

Amy realized now how Craig could have been at Helen's when Michael called. The voice had been on tape. Peter made the call from Craig's house, and activated the tape recorder.

If you need me, Doremus had said, *walk out on the quadrangle. Wear a pink sweater. I'll come on the run. It might take me ten minutes, twelve minutes ... I don't know. But I'll get there.*

211

After a while Amy lifted her head, listening. She had heard the two of them when they entered the building, but there hadn't been a sound since. Possibly they had gone upstairs to the infirmary.

She glanced at the pink sweater folded over the back of the chair behind her desk. Then she left the office without taking the sweater, walked nervelessly down the long hall. There were glimmerings of sun on the brown tile floor. She carried the key to Craig's office in one sweaty fist.

Craig had turned on the desk lamp and closed the blinds all the way. He sat behind the desk, his chair tipped back against the windowsill. There was a vertical line of strain between his eyes, but his voice was low, controlled. Peter sat nearby, in a high-backed wing chair, his feet on an ottoman. His head was tilted to one side and his eyes were closed. He had gone very easily into deep hypnotic sleep, in a matter of seconds. He had a curious, lifeless look, his skin waxen against the deep red of the leather chair.

"Your mother is there, Peter," Craig said, his eyes on the child's still face. "She's in the room with you. And you're happy to see her. Very happy. You're close to her. You love her very much."

Peter's eyelids fluttered, and his throat muscles worked. Gradually a smile appeared, but he lost his hold on it. He trembled, lightly, in his sleep. Craig leaned forward, worriedly.

"It's all right, Peter. You're with your mother, and everything is all right. You're going to speak to her today. You want very much to speak to her, to . . . tell her that you love her." Craig's voice weakened. "We only have . . . a little more time, Peter. Today you have to speak to her."

Noiselessly Craig rose from the chair and walked out from behind the desk. He stopped beside Peter's chair.

"Do you remember the sound of her voice? . . . Now she's speaking to you, Peter. What is she saying to you? Try to remember, try to tell me." He looked down tensely, waiting for a reaction. Peter's head rolled from side to side and his lips parted, but the only sound to escape him was a troubled sigh.

Outside, the wind had risen, driving leaves against the windows. Craig looked up distractedly, then returned his attention to Peter.

"Please try. Please speak to me."

The boy's back arched as if he were in pain. He fell back, groaning. But he said nothing.

Craig continued to watch Peter's face, intently and hopefully. Then his own throat muscles tightened. He rubbed his eyes remorsefully.

"You're not *trying*," he said brokenly. "Peter, you're . . ." The wind sighed, vibrating the glass of the windows. "Let's go back once more, to . . . to . . ." His mouth turned down petulantly. For a few moments there was sharp hatred in Craig's eyes. He reached suddenly, savagely, for Peter. The wind moaned, stopping him. Craig stepped back in fright. There was a roaring in his mind; the wind had become a bitter gale. He felt the barrenness of perpetual winter in his heart. His knees gave way and he slipped down beside the chair. In the horrid winter wastes of his heart a stricken eleven-year-old boy lived again. The cry from his heart was a cry of endless terror, or loss.

Michaeellll

"Michael," Craig said, writhing on the carpet. "Come back!"

He began crawling, slowly and torturously, sobbing in his throat. A few feet from the chair he toppled. His feet threshed against the carpet. Each violent breath knotted him. He was as speechless as Peter Mathis, who slept obliviously in the chair a few feet away. But, gradually, recognizable words were wrenched from his throat—adolescent, rambling phrases became clear, spoken in a high, youthful voice.

"Look what Mike made for you, Mother. I helped him. We went down to the creek today; you ought to see how full it is! There was a big black snake in a tree. Mike swam right under it and didn't see it. I held my breath under water a minute and a half. Mike counted . . ."

Before long he lay quietly on the soft carpet in the darkened room. Occasionally his chest heaved. He was quiet, but tension had scored his face. Then, abruptly, he sat up, listening, eyes alert. The sleeping boy attracted him. He walked over to the chair, looking grave and studious. When he spoke again his phrasing was that of an adult, but it was the same clear, childish voice.

"I know why you won't talk to me. I understand, Mike. I *let* them take Mother away." Craig's face darkened with resentment and hatred but he went on. "I found you, though. That's the important thing. We all thought you were gone, but I found out. You *will* speak to me again, won't you, Mike? Tonight. After the last one is dead."

He sat down behind the desk, a very purposeful eleven-year-old boy. "I saved her for last. I know you want to help me tonight, Michael. I know you want to help me kill her. Auntie Helen *hated* Mother. She really deserves to die. More than the others. She's going to get what's coming to her."

He was silent, thinking. "We'll call her on the phone again. I'll say ..." His voice went even higher, and his eyes widened in excitement. " 'Auntie Helen, this is Michael! I have to see you; a terrible thing is going to happen to Craig! Please come, I'm at Craig's house—please hurry.' " Craig shot a look at the sleeping boy, pleased with himself, and he giggled suddenly, covering his mouth with one hand. Then he reached out and turned on the tape recorder.

"*... king my mother, you're not ever going to get near her again you're not—*"

Craig hastily punched the button that stopped the tape; he sat stiffly for three or four seconds, staring at the machine. Fury reddened his eyes and he leaped from the chair in which he'd been sitting. The chair banged against the window-sill. Peter twitched in his sleep but his eyes remained closed. Craig raced for the office door, opened it.

The hallway outside was clear.

Craig made a savage sucking noise in his throat. For a few moments he felt dizzy. He leaned against the jamb, staring down the deserted hall. Midway there was a hot blaze of light: the westerly sun was shining through the glass of the entrance doors. The harsh light made Craig's eyes water. But he noticed something else at the far end of the hall, another vivid stripe of sun slashed diagonally across the dull brown tile. Almost as soon as he became aware of the stripe it vanished. A door had been quietly closed.

Something like a smile appeared on Craig's face, but his jaw muscles were rigid. He pulled the door of his office shut and began walking. Opposite the entrance he shielded his eyes from the glaring afternoon sun. Only a little of the fury had left his eyes. It made the clamped, jaw-breaking smile uniquely terrible.

When he reached Amy's office he didn't hesitate but yanked open the door and stepped inside. Amy was standing by her desk, visibly out of breath. Her head jerked around at his coming. She jumped half a foot.

Craig said, in his own voice. "You have a key to my office. I want it."

His eyes fumed, brooded. He stood slightly hunched, wolflike: he was totally unfamiliar. Amy tried to find something in him to respond to. She could do nothing but shake her head in weak protest.

Craig's smile faded. He moved closer, looking her over. Amy's right hand was clenched on the desk top.

He said offhandedly, "You're a no-good goddamned whore. You know that, don't you?"

Amy's breath hissed. She had been prepared for anything but indignity, humiliation. The slap of it gave her new life, a flickering of courage. "Why? Why am I that?" Her eyes were steady on him; tears formed in them. "Because I . . . loved you?"

"Give me the key or I'll break your hand."

Amy turned her hand over and the key rang on the glass surface of the desk. "Here. Take your key. Craig, I want . . . I want very much to talk to you. Will you sit down?"

Craig's eyes darted to the key. His smile came and went. He reached for the key. She wasn't watching; she was still looking at his face. His hand paused above the key, then closed on a baseball-size glass paperweight with a gorgeous orange-and-black butterfly inside.

Amy touched his left-hand sleeve, imploringly. "Craig, it's so important that we—"

He hit her, somewhat awkwardly, over the left ear with the heavy paperweight. Amy made a meaningless sound in her throat and buckled. As she went down her hands tightened on his jacket. Her eyes opened partway and she looked up at him, dazed.

Craig was bent by the strength of her hands. "I don't *want* to talk to you," he said earnestly, his voice high. He swung the paperweight again, from above the head. In the golden dusty silence of the little office the paperweight made a brutal rapping sound on the flat of Amy's skull. She slid limply to the floor. There was a red seeping at the roots of her blond hair.

Craig looked at her for perhaps half a minute. He set the paperweight aside, picked Amy up in his arms, grunted, threw her down again on the carpet behind her desk. He stood back, near the door. One of her legs from the knee down was visible protruding from behind the desk. He returned and bent the leg at the knee until it was hidden. He looked once more at her dry white face, bluish around the eyes, hollow in the temples. He had hit her very hard and he didn't know if she was breathing or not. He had no desire to find out.

He let himself out of the office and walked slowly down the hall, shambling a little, not picking up his feet.

Peter was in the same position in the wine-red high-backed chair, his small-boned hands slack in his lap. Craig squatted beside the chair, he ran his hand lightly, sympathetically over the head of the sleeper. Peter sighed, fitfully.

"I'm sorry, Michael," Craig whispered. "I'm sorry you have to go out tonight. But it's necessary."

16

Doremus had chosen a place high on the razor-back, almost directly above the school. There had been a minor rock slide in the area a year ago, clearing brush and loose soil, so nothing interfered with his line of sight. He sat with his back against an old elm tree with half its roots exposed where the slide had pared the declivity to clean rock. His booted feet were braced against one of the dry roots. He had left his 30-.06 rifle and his Dayglo-orange vest and deer hunter's cap home, but otherwise he was dressed exactly as he would have been on a hunt, for comfort and warmth. The wind sometimes howled just above his head but he had chosen his stand well—often during the long day he was afraid he had chosen too well: he was far too comfortable and battling the urge to sleep.

Hourly he arose and pulled himself up to level

ground and walked around to get the kinks out of his knees and loosen stiffened muscles, then clambered down to resume his wait. He had a pair of 7×50 Japanese-made binoculars around his neck. His cache included a stock of cigars and a quart canteen of water. He also had a compact Citizens' Band radio along; he had used it twice, the first time around noon when he observed Amy Lawlor's car entering the school grounds. The second time had been at sundown, and he'd had nothing of interest to report. Both Amy's Mustang and Craig's Chevelle were still parked behind the administration building. He had seen neither of them all afternoon, and he was worried about that.

The faint steady hum of the CB radio was interrupted by Enoch Mills' voice.

"Doremus?"

He reached down and picked up the radio microphone. "Right here."

"I make it ten after nine. Anything stirring?"

"No. Peter and Craig apparently had dinner in Craig's office . . . I saw a tray being carried over. Then Peter left the administration building, alone, at seven, and walked across the quadrangle to his hall. I suppose he's in bed. The lights in Dobbs went out on schedule, and Franklin Hall should go dark in five minutes. As far as I know, Craig is still in his office."

"What about the girl? She was only going to be there an hour at the most."

Doremus hesitated; he had thought about little else during the past few hours. "I don't know where she is. I've had the glasses on her office window but I can't tell a thing. There aren't any lights."

"She must have run into trouble then. I think we ought to move in."

"If she's in trouble, that might make it worse. And if she's . . . dead, then we're too late already. I have a feeling something's about to happen, otherwise Craig would have gone home by now. Let's give him a little more time."

For the next hour Doremus kept the binoculars to his eyes almost continuously, lowering them only when the strain became intolerable and his vision blurred. He chewed nervously on an unlighted cigar, deeply regretting his decision to let Amy prowl through Craig's office on the chance that she might come across something they could use against him. *Otherwise he's going to be hurt, isn't he? Maybe he'll be killed. Please let me give it a try, Doremus.*

Damned fool, he thought, referring to himself. She'd been getting by on raw nerve alone, but he'd let her convince him. In a way he had handed Amy right over to that maniac. He hurled the sodden cigar over the cliff. *She isn't hurt and she isn't dead*, he told himself, trying to ease his conscience. *The odds are Craig surprised her in his office this afternoon and he's holding her. But that means he's going to be approximately twice as tough to get to.* He rubbed his smarting eyes. *Soft in the head, Doremus. Soft like a melon. If you'd stayed on the force you'd be directing traffic in a cemetery right now. So think of something.*

The sound of the school bell drifted through the wind; it tolled ten times. Doremus lifted his binoculars and began a thorough end-to-end check of the quiet campus. He was able to see the night watchman in his booth by the gates. Reading a newspaper. He hadn't looked out all night. If the gymnasium fell down he'd find out about it from the papers.

Tree shadows danced in the circles of light on the quadrangle. He turned the glasses on the dark bulk of the residence halls. He could not see the inner windows but the slant of the roof shone in the moonlight, gunmetal gray. He traced the roof line, focused for a few moments on the black half-acre of parking lot, the delivery area and loading dock behind the cafeteria. There was a stabbing pain in his left shoulder he hadn't been able to work out. He ignored it, returned his attention to the roof of Dobbs Hall.

The boy had appeared there as if conjured. He stood, motionless, straight, assured, in the moonlight. Doremus felt his throat squeezing tight. For several seconds Peter seemed to be listening, to be looking for something. A gust of wind almost unbalanced him. He recovered, then began running, nimbly, across the tar-and-gravel surface. Doremus tracked him, marveling. When he reached the limit of the roof Peter leaned momentarily over the parapet, looking down at the vertical mat of ivy on the otherwise blank wall.

"Watch yourself, kid," Doremus said under his breath. "Maybe you've done it before, but take care."

Confidently the boy climbed over the two-foot-high parapet, held on with both hands while he dug with his toes into the tough vine. Doremus couldn't tell if he was wearing sneakers. When he seemed sure of a foothold Peter started down. It was difficult to follow his progress, even with the good binoculars, because of the dark background. It seemed to take him the better part of five minutes to go just a few feet.

Quite suddenly, as Doremus watched edgily, Peter appeared to lose his grip, or perhaps the vine pulled away from the wall. He was free of the wall, falling. Doremus leaned forward, helplessly. Peter landed on his feet on the covered walkway to the cafeteria, swayed there, took a hasty step to steady himself. It looked as if he would fall again, head-first to the asphalt parking strip. But he regained balance and went down on one knee to catch his breath.

The rest of the way down was easy for him: an eight-foot jump to a grassy terrace. He picked himself up, vanished beneath the walkway. Doremus tried vainly for a couple of minutes to pick him up again. When he had his next glimpse of Peter, the boy was running at the edge of the drive, circling behind the administration building. Doremus turned the binoculars on the Chevelle. Craig was standing beside it, waiting.

He spoke to Peter, briefly, dropping a hand on his shoulder. Then he opened a door of the car and Peter got in. Instead of getting into the car himself, Craig walked briskly back to the building. Doremus lost him. He lowered the glasses for a few moments to give his eyes a rest. Apparently there was a back entrance, most probably a basement entrance. The angle was wrong and he couldn't find a doorway with his glasses.

Automatically Doremus looked at the glowing face of his chronometer: nine minutes past ten. He raised the binoculars again.

At twenty after, Craig reappeared, carrying Amy.

The distance was too great for Doremus to tell what condition she was in, or if she was bound. Craig held her with one arm while he lifted the lid

223

of the trunk. Unhappily there was no revealing flash of light from inside the trunk. But judging from the loose way she sprawled when Craig put her inside, she was at least unconscious, if not dead. The hatred he felt for Craig Young was as blinding as a migraine headache. He reached down, groped for the CB radio, put it in his lap. He kept his eyes on the Chevelle while he brought Enoch Mills in.

"We've got some action. Also complications. Craig's about to leave the school. Peter Mathis is in the back seat of the car, probably lying flat so he won't be seen when Craig drives through the gate. And Amy is in the trunk."

"What shape is she in?"

"I don't know. Half an hour closed up in that trunk and she's a goner no matter what. OK, he's just leaving the grounds. Better have the boys in the other car close slow. No lights. He may be panicky."

"We're ready for him," Enoch said crisply. "Come a runnin'."

Doremus clutched the radio in one hand and pulled himself up the slope. When he was standing, he unclipped the flashlight from his belt and cut his way through the buckbrush with it. Twenty yards away was an old logging road, a barely passable slash up the wooded spine of the razorback. He would never have gotten a car up there and in fact he'd had to push his scooter part of the way, but he anticipated only moderate difficulty going down. He stowed the radio away, fixed the lamp to the handlebars for additional light, kicked the motor to life and went charging away, head low to avoid the unexpected lash of a low-hanging limb.

He'd had no way of timing it, but he thought it should take him no more than four minutes to reach the base of the ridge, where the hardtop road out of Eveningshade Hollow curved sharply around, continued on into the village two miles away. Mills had set up his intercept point there.

There were two of them, out of uniform, in an unmarked car. Engine trouble; the car was blocking the road. Mills would wave Craig down, approach apologetically, put the light and his gun on Craig at the same time. Maybe it would work. Or maybe Craig wouldn't slow down at all, and kill a couple of people trying to run away. He might have a gun of his own. But they had talked it over and decided it was the best way to grab him without unnecessary risks.

If he's driving slow, Doremus thought, plummeting toward the valley on the atrocious road, his no longer young bones taking a pounding, *if he's driving slow and watching the bad curves in that road and maybe talking to Peter, then I've got a one-minute lead on him. Time to ditch the scooter and dig in by the side of the road with the Woodsman. Just in case it takes three men.* But he wasn't planning to mix in. It was up to Mills now. Craig probably wouldn't recognize the undersheriff right away, not without his uniform.

The road turned down so steeply he thought he was going to go headfirst over the handlebars, and he lost his seat momentarily. Then the road widened, became level, and he went rocketing through a grove of young trees.

That girl, he thought. *I don't believe I could forgive myself if—*He brought the scooter to a skidding stop, parked it, ran for the blacktop road, pulling the Colt from his waistband. He saw the sheriff's car just before the big curve, taillights glowing. The deputy was under the hood with a flashlight. He had a sawed-off shotgun in his other hand. Mills leaned against the side of his car, a big white Pontiac. The beam of his flashlight circled lazily on the road. He turned his head as Doremus approached, gasping for breath.

"Likely spot there," he said, pointing. "Good cover; he won't pick you up in his headlights."

"As soon as you pull him out of the car I'll go for the boy."

"Fine idea."

"How far behind him are your boys?"

"Reckon about a thousand yards. He won't know they're there, but if he tries to back off on us they'll block him right quick."

"Well, he's due," Doremus said. Except for the toneless wind moan, the night was still. Early frost had driven cicadas and tree frogs into the mud, and they were not close to farms or houses and the inevitable dogs. Doremus went down on his elbows below the road.

Three more minutes passed. Mills shuffled his feet on the asphalt and spat. The deputy said hoarsely, "Where's he at?"

"Maybe he had a flat tire," Mills said. "Hold it!"

Doremus looked up. A squad car came slowly into view, lights out.

"Be damned," Mills said sullenly, and wagged his flashlight. The squad car speeded up and jerked to a stop near him. Doremus got slowly to his feet. The deputy driving the squad car stuck his head out the window and said:

"Thought you'd have him. Where'd he go?"

"You tell me."

Doremus said, "You didn't pass him on the road?"

"Hell, no."

"Where could he have pulled off?" Doremus asked Mills.

"I don't know. Chuck, bring me the map."

The other two deputies remained in the squad car with the engine idling. The driver switched on his headlights as Mills unfolded the big Geological Survey map of Shades County on the trunk of his Pontiac.

"Here's the only access road between this point and the school," he muttered, aiming his flashlight at one grid of the map. "It's dirt, winds down across Settler Creek and through this bottom land, past a good-sized gravel pit. Comes out a quarter mile from the Big Diamond truck stop on 60."

"Then he's on that road."

"Could be. Only thing is, we've had the road partially barricaded almost six months now. Spring flood weakened the bridge across the creek there. It's just before falling down. He's bound to know that."

"What if he tried to get across the bridge?"

Chuck said, "What's he driving? A compact? There's a chance he might get across. He'd be a damned fool to try though. Why do you suppose he turned off the hard road?"

"Something made him nervous. Or maybe he meant to all the time. He might be looking for a place to—" Mills glanced up at Doremus with a hint of shock in his green eyes.

"To drop a body off," Doremus said, finishing it for him.

"That gravel pit would be ideal," Mills admitted. "But there's other places he could do it, and she might not be found for a while." The map bellied as the wind blew hard and Mills had to hold it down with both hands.

"It's also possible he pulled off behind the barricade and stopped there with his lights off," Doremus speculated. "Because . . . say he needed a couple of minutes to think something over. Maybe Amy is alive after all, and she was making noises in the trunk. Or he could have left something he needs at the school. If he was on the dirt road then he'd have seen the squad car go by with all lights out and become damned suspicious. That might have prompted him to double back this way." Doremus traced the Eveningshade Hollow road east, past the school and around the other end of the razorback. "If he did that, then he has a choice of roads by now. He could be anywhere."

Mills walked back to the squad car and spoke briefly to his boys. The driver turned the car around and they went off with a quick screech of tires.

"Told Bryant and McLemore to look for him this side of the bridge," Mills explained when he returned, "and I said if they was to see him then they should take him. If he ain't on the dirt road they'll make a circuit of the school grounds. Then they'll cruise all the roads between Constable Ridge and Blounstown. They won't try to take him if the car's moving though—too much chance of an accident and the Mathis boy maybe getting hurt. Meantime I want to go down by the gravel pit. I've got it in my head that's where he is this minute, hauling that poor girl out of the trunk of his car. You ridin' with us, Doremus?"

"No."

Mills gave him a long look. "What are you thinking?"

"I'm wondering what Craig did to Amy. Did he make her tell that he was being watched? His actions so far indicate both carelessness and deep suspicion. What's going on in his mind? So far we've more or less assumed that he's rational, we've been trying to guess what a sane man with a body on his hands might do. But suppose he's broken down completely. He might have forgotten Amy's back there in the trunk. He might be driving around in the moonlight talking to himself with spit on his chin. He might not have any idea of where he is, what time it is, or whether he's hot or cold. Then again he could be going step by step through some intricate plot that only makes a little bit of sense to a logical mind and is guaranteed to drive us crazy trying to figure it out. And while we go off in all directions he's gradually working his way around to another victim: Helen."

"I could sure use some more men," Mills said with a sigh. "What the hell do we do? Stake out the Connelly house?"

"Not just yet. I imagine we've got an hour or two before Craig gets to Helen. In the meantime I think you ought to keep Bryant and the other deputy cruising. Who knows, they might find Craig pulled off by the side of the road somewhere reciting nursery rhymes. You might come across him sitting at the edge of the gravel pit counting bubbles where Amy sank." His forehead was deeply ridged. "I think we ought to spread out but be prepared to close quickly when Craig gives notice. I'm going to ride my scooter into the village. Helen was planning to take Peggy and me to the movies tonight—before I was called out of town, that is—and I might find them at the theater. Unfortunately it's time to bring her up to date on nephew Craig."

In the village he found the theater dark; the evening show had let out at ten. For that matter the downtown area was nearly deserted, with only two places of business open. They were both taprooms, one at each end of the main street.

There was a phone booth at the Gulf station two blocks north of the courthouse, so he got back on his scooter and went popping around the corner. By his chronometer it was ten minutes of eleven. Exactly half an hour since Craig had put Amy in the trunk of his car. In Doremus' mind there was a vivid chilling image: Craig aimlessly driving and driving on the back roads of Shades County, driving long past the moment when Amy would take the last breath of foul trunk air and die. He discovered he was shaking, his bones ached. He gritted his teeth and parked the scooter next to the lighted phone booth and dialed Helen Connelly's number.

After he'd listened to a dozen rings he began sweating coldly.

On the eighteenth ring Peggy answered, yawning at the same time. "H'lo."

"Peggy, this is Doremus."

"It is?" she said doubtfully.

"Yes. I'm back in The Shades now. Could I talk to your mother, please?"

"OK," Peggy said, and Doremus heard the receiver bump as she put it down on the table. *Mother! Doremus wants to talk to you!*

Doremus leaned against one side of the booth, his eyes watering from strain. He fumbled in his shirt pocket for his Polaroid sunglasses and put them on. Two minutes passed; he couldn't hear Peggy anymore. Fear struck at the back of his neck, spread a swift paralysis down his spine.

"Peggy," he shouted into the receiver. "Peggy, do you hear me?"

Rigidly he waited another half minute; then, with a shock of relief, he heard her on the other end of the wire.

"I don't think she's here," Peggy said, uncertainly.

"Go to the door," he said, trying to keep his voice from betraying anxiety. "Look out and see if your mother's wagon is parked by the street."

"I can see from here," Peggy said. "It's gone. Where did Mother go, Doremus?"

"I ... I don't think she went very far. Look, honey, do me a favor right now. I want you to go into the office as soon as you hang up and lock the door behind you. Make sure you lock the door, now. Wait there. Wait until Sheriff Mills comes. He'll be there in just a few minutes, and he'll call to you loud enough for you to hear. But don't ... don't let anybody else in the house. Do you understand? Not even Craig. Stay in the office with the door locked. Even if you hear Craig calling you, don't go out."

"Why?"

"It's important, Peg. I'll explain later, when I see you. That'll be soon. In the meantime, promise me you'll wait in the office for the sheriff?"

"Yes," Peggy said, as if she thought it was all rather silly. "Good-bye."

As soon as he had hung up Doremus retrieved the CB radio from his Cushman. "Mills!"

"This is Mills. What's up?"

"Where are you now?"

"Headed south on 22. We'll be at the gravel pit in about another four minutes."

"Can you turn around and get over to the Connellys'? I just talked to Peggy. She's alone there. Apparently Helen left her sleeping in her room and went off in a hurry somewhere; the ranch wagon is gone."

"Turn us around, Chuck," the sheriff said in an aside to his deputy. To Doremus he said, "Where do you suppose she went?"

"I don't know. She must have been convinced it was urgent; otherwise she wouldn't have left Peggy like that—particularly after I warned her. I think Craig got her out of the house."

"You suppose he's after the kid instead of Helen?" Dimly Doremus heard the screeching of tires as the deputy made a looping turn.

"He might be. I told Peggy to lock herself into the first-floor office and not open up for anybody but you. Holler loud when you hit the front porch."

"We can pick you up at 22 and White Church."

"No, I'm going to try to track Helen down."

"On that scooter? Let me get Bryant and McLemore over to you. Where you calling from?"

Doremus rubbed his forehead in agitation. "I've had a lot of sour hunches in the last three-quarters of an hour. I'd made up my mind that Craig was just driving around in a daze. I don't believe it now. He knows exactly what he's doing; he's working according to a timetable and so far everything's clicking nicely for him. Here's the last of my hunches, and God help the Connellys if I'm wrong. Craig isn't interested in Peggy, it's Helen he wants. He's lured her to a dark and private place where he plans to kill her."

"What place?"

"Two choices. He's had a fondness for the burned-out house where he and his brother lived; he's taken Peter there before. According to his logic it might be the ideal setting to complete his cycle of revenge. It would take me half an hour to get there on my scooter though. Bryant and Mc-Lemore can make it in half the time."

"I'll contact them. Where are you headed?"

"Up Ben Lomond. Craig might have done the most predictable thing of all—driven straight home and called Helen from there. I know approximately where his house is, what it looks like. I can get up there in ten minutes."

"We'll be right behind you," Mills promised.

"Let me try it alone. He may be watching for a car and before you could get close he'd kill her, if he hasn't already. But a man on a motor scooter without lights isn't that easy to see, and he'll never hear me in this wind. Give me . . . half an hour. I think I can surprise him."

There were few houses on Ben Lomond Mountain, because the solitary switchback road that went two and a quarter miles to the primitive little state park at the summit was paved only with gravel and subject to both slides and washouts. Those who lived there used up a new car on the steeps and binds of the road roughly at the rate of one every ten months. They were forced to pump most of their water up the side of the mountain or collect rainwater in cisterns. But the majority of the houses were elaborate, and the owners were repaid for their trouble and the expense of building in such isolation by staggering views of the Ozark plateau and the national forests in the area.

Craig had been living for the better part of two years in a house he rented from a man named Dillbeck, who had been both a governor and a United States senator until an upset victory by a wellheeled Republican had retired him from public office at the age of fifty-five. He had scarcely moved into his retirement house, which had taken months to build, when he was offered a choice assignment as an ambassador at large by his old buddy the President. Consequently he hadn't set foot in the state for over a year.

The house occupied a teetering acre fifty feet from the upward swing of the road. There was a stretch of redwood fence with white brick posts by the road. You turned in off the gravel onto a stretch of blacktop, passed through heavy solid gates. The drive was like a big comma wedged between the house and a side of the mountain that went almost straight up, with outcroppings of limestone. All the level space behind the modern California-style house was paved, and there was room for three cars to maneuver. The subtly pitched roof of the house, surfaced with white crushed stone, rose only a few feet above the asphalt, and the long white brick wall was without windows. The way into the house was through a door in another redwood fence, this one six feet high.

Helen drove haltingly through the gates and into the parking area, unnerved as always by the drive up, unnerved by the telephone call, the Michael call that had prompted her to grab her purse and coat and run from the house unthinkingly. She wondered now why she hadn't tried to contact the sheriff first—but there hadn't seemed to be any time at all. She had been afraid for Craig's life.

His car was there, facing the road. She pulled up behind it, got out. The wind tore at her hair, deafened her. She took three unsteady steps toward the house, head down. She didn't realize she had left the headlights of the car turned on.

The wind slackened suddenly and it was like being released from the drag of a rope. She threw out a hand, bracing herself against the rough wall of the house. Then the wind whipsawed her again. She stumbled on to the high door in the fence, wondering how Craig could live up here, with the constant wind scream.

Craig, she thought, tingling, half-panicked. She fought with the wind-guarded door, propped it open, stepped inside. Here it was quieter. She glanced at the curtained window wall that extended almost the length of the house. No lights were visible.

"Craig!"

There were two flights of steps, one ascending to a long roofed gallery, the other descending. She looked out over the tiered Japanese garden, at shaky rare evergreens, tall swaying trees, squat, tormented-looking trees. Lighted, the garden had a stylized beauty. But it was dark now, except for the recurring moon. Shadows leaped against the wall at her back.

"Where are you, Craig?"

The wind slowed; almost beside her she heard a childish giggling and she turned her head sharply.

A boy in cowboy clothes was standing there: big red Stetson-type hat tied under his chin, an imitation-leather vest with a shiny star pinned to it, imitation-fur chaps. He was pointing a silvery revolver at her.

He giggled again, and snapped off three rapid shots from the cap pistol. Helen nearly fell off the rock path to the iron stairs below. When she recovered he was gone: he had jumped nimbly from the ledge to a terrace of the garden. She could not find him in the tossing shadows. And then she had a glimpse of his red hat as he peered out at her from behind a square-trimmed shrub.

"Come here," she made herself say. "I want you to . . . Who are you?" She knew who it must be, but she couldn't think of a name. Not Michael though. Certainly not Michael. Her relief was distinct, warming. This was a real boy, playing a boy's game, he was not Michael.

But Michael had called her.

Helen started down to the first level of the garden, began walking to her left, toward the place where she had seen him. She was holding her hands to her ears, trying to shut out the incessant wind. She saw him again.

Popping up one level down, from the shadows of a plumelike waving tree that grew twenty feet tall.

"Come here . . . please come here! I want to talk to you! Where's Craig?" She stopped and looked hopefully at the house. But it was completely dark. *Why?* she wondered. A hard wave of fear almost toppled her.

"Boy," she shouted, and his name came to her tongue. "Peter! Quit playing now. I have to talk to you."

There was a lull; she heard the popping of the

cap gun. Turning quickly, she saw him run from one place of concealment to another.

Helen followed. She was in the midst of the garden now, surrounded by all the carefully nurtured oddities foreign to the soil of Missouri. Above the wind a few stars glimmered undisturbed. She went on, searching carefully.

Out of the tail of her eyes she saw something move on the gallery of the house. Helen stared, trying to make out what it was. . . . A dog? But a dog wouldn't move so awkwardly. She was drawn closer to the gallery. Behind her the little boy giggled; she was absorbed and horrified by the creeping shape on the gallery and didn't bother to turn around.

"Craig?" Helen said, once again. The thing stopped. Helen walked to within a few feet of the gallery, but she still couldn't see what it was. Then she realized that it must be Craig, on all fours.

He's hurt, she thought, and started for the stairs.

Behind her there was a throaty, drawn-out shriek. The sound he was making numbed her as thoroughly as an electric shock. It seemed to take all of a minute for her to look around, to look up at him.

He was standing, fully visible against the dark-gray and star-shot sky. Helen saw that he wore almost no clothes, but nothing else could really surprise her because he was still shrieking. Her tongue felt bolted to the roof of her mouth and her heart was like a tight little sack of broken glass. Vaguely she recognized the fierce and terrifying cries. She had heard them in a good many western movies just before the Indians swooped down and slaughtered all of the homesteaders.

Unconsciously her mouth curled in an expression very like a smile, but she felt no laughter.

With ceremonial slowness Craig raised his right hand, raised it high. He was holding a thick-bladed knife almost ten inches long.

He came down then, with a step and a leap and another whoop, and crouched within five feet of her. She saw, more or less clearly, the dark stripings of paint on his naked chest and face. Her vision blurred momentarily, and then she focused on the hunting knife. As astounded as she was, Helen felt a definite fearful shriveling inside.

Enough, she wanted to say. *Don't anymore. Stop now. It isn't funny any more.* And even as she was thinking this she realized with a horrid certainty that it wasn't a joke. He was going to kill her.

Doremus had come through the gates in a boil of black smoke and seen Helen's car, with headlights blazing, parked behind the Chevelle. His ears throbbed from the howl of wind and the racket of the failing scooter engine. He pulled up beside Craig's car, put the kickstand down with his foot and went for the trunk of the Chevelle. It wasn't locked.

Amy lay cramped inside, jackknifed, her back to him. There were streaks that could have been blood or grease in her blond hair. He found it difficult to free her because he was afraid to exert much force. He got one hand under a shoulder and another under her thighs and tugged gently, then turned her and lifted her out. Amy's head fell back and he looked at her besmirched, oddly flat-looking face. He could not tell if she had suffocated there in the trunk. Her skin was cool to the touch.

He heard Helen scream, somewhere.

Doremus took two quick steps, wrenched open one of the doors of the Chevelle and laid Amy inside on the seat, face up. He closed the door, stepped back, drew the Colt automatic from his waistband and looked the house over. At first he couldn't see a way in. He heard Helen screaming again and then a series of flat cracking sounds, like undernourished firecrackers, or . . .

Cap pistol? he thought, and ran toward the fence. When he was on top of it he saw the outline of the door.

There seemed to be no one in the garden, but as he tried to orient himself the wind let up and the trees fell to quaking lightly; shadows froze. Then he could see them all, Peter in his cowboy suit and Craig—apparently—in his birthday suit. They were at the bottom of the sheltered garden, close to a low retaining wall of rock. Helen had fallen and she was trying to rise from her knees. She sobbed hysterically. Craig stood two or three feet behind her, hands at his sides: Doremus thought he heard a high-pitched and excited child's voice. Peter was farther away, on a tier above them, cap pistol in hand.

As Doremus watched, the knife in Craig's hand flashed up and he bent over his Aunt Helen. She looked back, screamed again. Instinctively Doremus raised his Colt, sighting. Then two things happened, quickly, confusingly. The wind tugged at his out-stretched hand, spoiling his aim, and Peter, who had been motionless and absorbed, moved into the line of fire.

Doremus screamed, "Get out of there! Peter, move!"

Even as he said it Peter hurtled from the tier he

had been standing on and landed, like a trained monkey, on Craig's back. Craig was staggered, but the knife slashed down and Helen pitched forward on her face. From where he was standing Doremus could not see if Craig had hit her with the blade. He began to run, recklessly, down the shallow garden steps.

"Mike," Craig said, in his childish voice, "get off, Mike! Let me finish!" He lunged to his feet, brushing the boy off his back; he made a quick move with his knife hand in the direction of the prostrate woman. But just as quickly Peter grabbed him around the legs, held him back. Craig tried to kick free. Peter was sobbing.

"Don't!" Peter said. "Don't hurt! Don't don't don't."

Craig lifted his head and saw Doremus coming. With a violent kick he sent Peter flying against the rock wall and dashed in the direction of the house. As soon as Craig detached himself from Peter, Doremus risked a shot, snapping it, but Craig was quick and the bullet went behind him.

Doremus continued on to the bottom of the garden and the paved walk there, knelt beside Helen. She was unconscious. He lifted her by one shoulder, saw the dark oozing wound, high, two or three inches from the base of her neck. Peter sat rubbing his head slowly, in a dazed way.

"From now on you're the sheriff," Doremus said to him, handing over the cap pistol Peter had dropped. He looked up and saw Craig midway on the gallery, running hard, bent over. Doremus lifted the Colt, led him, squeezed off a shot that nicked concrete ahead of the nearly naked man. He put another one into the redwood fence an instant after Craig opened the high door and escaped.

Doremus followed, missed a step, fell hard on the rough stone, tearing the knee out of his hunting pants, lacerating the palm of one hand. He scrambled up, unnecessarily furious with himself for having missed two chancy shots with an unfamiliar handgun. He tried running but had to adjust to a fast limping walk.

When he was still ten feet from the fence he heard the engine of the Chevelle turn over, roar loudly, heard the tires laying down rubber as Craig gunned away with the brakes on. Doremus wondered bleakly what he had been thinking about, putting Amy in that car. It had seemed like a good idea, but he should have taken the trouble to pull the keys from the ignition first.

The Chevelle tires were still peeling on the blacktop when another set of tires yelped and the night split open as two cars collided, ripping each other fender to fender. Doremus reached the open door in the gate as Enoch Mills' car came lurching into view, one headlight glaring angrily. They had met at the driveway gates, where there was room for only a car and a half. Craig's Chevelle had veered several feet to the right, knocked down one of the brick posts and torn up several feet of valuable fencing before coming to a complete stop. For a few moments, in the wind lull, there was no sound but the hiss of escaping steam from the radiator of the sheriff's car; then the mashed door on the driver's side opened with a deadly grinding noise and the deputy named Chuck stepped out uncertainly, clutching his left arm below the elbow. He took two weaving steps, dropped to his knees, rolled slowly over, one cheek resting on the cold asphalt.

Doremus limped to the other side of the wrecked Pontiac, opened the door. Enoch Mills had pulled himself off the padded dash. There was a trace of blood on his mouth, and his lower lip appeared to be split. He shook his head a couple of times, sorrowfully, looked at Doremus.

"We come a little early," he explained.

Doremus helped him out. "I'm all right," Mills said. "What happened to Chuck?"

"Passed out." They both started around the car toward the fallen deputy. Doremus saw the smoke around the Chevelle then. He took a step in the direction of the other car, hesitated. Craig Young stumbled out of the hovering gray smoke, came straight at them. For a few moments the red streaks of paint on his face hid the fact that he was bleeding from the left temple. But he had held on to his knife somehow.

Doremus centered the muzzle of his automatic on Craig's heaving chest. "Throw it down," he said softly.

Craig stopped abruptly, looked at the two men with suspicion. He raised the knife a couple of inches, threateningly. Doremus calmly thumbed back the hammer of the Colt.

"What the hell," Mills said, staring. "Where's his clothes?"

"Brave warriors don't wear clothes. Right, Craig? Oh, your Aunt Helen's OK. You only got her in the shoulder. Now let's put the knife down and play some other game for a while; this one's been a little hard on everybody."

Blood dripped from Craig's left cheekbone. His lips parted and he showed his teeth. Doremus noted that he had shaved off the manly moustache. Without it his face looked thinner, flayed to the bone. Doremus could almost see Craig's heart beating through the ridged wall of his chest. The blood seemed to be flowing more profusely from the wound at his temple. Doremus felt a tug of pity for him, wondering at the same time if Sheriff Washbrook had seen something like this just before he was killed.

"One more time, Craig. The knife." He had the unhappy feeling that he was going to be forced to kill Craig, and he was already planning how to do it with a minimum of distress. At that range he knew he could not miss the heart, and Craig would be dead in the blink of an eye. But weariness befuddled him; for a couple of seconds the barrel of the automatic dipped.

Craig jumped at them, screaming, and hurled his knife. It hit Enoch Mills butt first over the left eye and he went over backward as if he'd been slugged. Instead of following the knife and charging, Craig whirled and made for the limestone cliff across the drive. Doremus aimed the automatic reluctantly. Then, as Craig began climbing, he put the Colt away and helped Mills to his feet.

"Where's he going?" Mills said, fingering the sore spot on his forehead.

"I don't think he knows. Up. Out, maybe. But he won't make it."

They watched silently as Craig continued to climb, frantically. They could hear him grunting, scrabbling with his fingernails. Small rocks rained on the blacktop. He was thirty feet up, looking pale and fragile against the cliff, when he began to falter. He pressed in, gripping the rock with every inch of his skinny body. The wind was troubling him. They heard him cry out, unintelligibly. Then he went on.

"I don't know if I can watch it," Mills muttered. He hauled Chuck off the paving, carried him to the Pontiac, which was tilted over a flattened tire, and put him in. Then he took his CB radio off the floor, tested it. Doremus stayed where he was, looking up. It was harder to see Craig now, but he could still be heard; each agonized breath cut through the dull sweep of the wind.

And then he came down in a shower of soft broken rock, came down like a featherless bird, arms outflung, still reaching for the last handhold. He hit the asphalt drive feet first, at a slight angle, collapsed, his head bounding as it struck an instant later. He lay still and foreshortened and the stripes of red war paint gleamed in the light from the Pontiac.

Doremus heard a grating noise and looked at the Chevelle. There was still smoke around it, as from burned brakes. The right-side door had opened and he saw a pair of hands, a straggly blond head. She came crawling determinedly out, stood up, wobbled, leaned against the roof of the Chevelle. She looked at the splintered fence and the rubble at her feet and then toward him, blindly. Doremus wondered how he could have forgotten all about Amy.

"Would somebody please help me?" she asked in a timid voice.

He was there in plenty of time to grab her before the wobble could get any worse.

17

The soft sound of the sea uncurling against the narrow strip of sand beach a few yards away from the honeymoon cottage awakened her, as it usually did, shortly after dawn. She floated, delightfully, for another ten minutes between sleep and full awareness before edging out of bed.

The air-conditioner was off but there was a slight chill in the bedroom and she remembered it had rained during the night. She stripped off the filmy trifle of a nightgown in which she had slept, letting it drift to the rumpled king-size bed. She looked with a trace of a smile where Doremus had slept for a few hours before the thought of uncaught fish out there in the sea had raised him and sent him stumbling off in the black of night with half-opened eyes. She shook her head at this unshakable dedication and went into the bathroom for a five-minute shower.

Afterward, smiling to herself, she chose light-blue shorts and a bright Jamaica print blouse, dressed, slipped her feet into Italian sandals and went out on the porch. The sun was behind her, its heat not apparent yet, but the sky had turned blue. The precisely clipped grass of the lawn and the fronds of the two palms were still beaded from the rain. Out on the placid water there was a long low boat with two men in it. She thought she recognized her husband and smiled again.

A tall, white-coated waiter came down the walk, carefully balancing a breakfast tray on his head. He stepped onto the porch, put the tray on a glass-topped coffee table. "Good morning, mum."

"Good morning, Jonas."

"How's the sunburn today? Not so bad, I see."

She looked down at her peeling thighs ruefully. "Much better. I thought I could take sun very well, so I'm afraid I was careless."

"Oh, mum, Jamaica sun is fierce all the year round. But you luckier than other ladies; some actually go to the hospital from the sunburn. You have plenty more time to enjoy your stay."

"Yes," she said, her eyes returning to the boat, which was now shorebound. "I am luckier than other ladies."

He finished setting the table with crisp linen and laid out their breakfast, then went striding back to the hotel two blocks away, the now empty tray under his arm. She poured a cup of hot coffee for herself, stood with a hip against one post of the porch, watching the boat come in. When the two men were close to shore and she could see they had a catch, she ran past the little emerald-shaped swimming pool and went down to the beach. Doremus, wearing boat shoes, swim trunks and a straw hat, was in the water, helping the guide beach the boat.

"What have you got?" she said, and he flashed a smile. The guide, whose name was Freddy, bobbed his head excitedly. "Shark, mum. Shark."

Water lapped over her toes and she took a hurried step back. "What?"

"Mako shark," Doremus said, reaching into the boat for it.

She peered closely at the mako, and was disappointed. It resembled pictures of sharks which she'd seen, but it was only about three feet long. "Aren't you supposed to throw back the babies?" she said.

Doremus laughed. "This is as long as they get. Want to see his teeth?"

"Ecch. Wait, let me get the camera. Even if it is a baby I want a picture." She ran back to the house, scooped up the Polaroid someone had given them as a wedding present, paused to pour her husband some coffee and ran back to the beach, arriving out of breath. She made them both pose with the shark. Then Freddy put it back in the boat and pushed off from shore.

"Tomorrow," he said cheerfully, "I find us a whole school of bonita."

"I'm counting on you, Freddy." They went leisurely back to the cottage, and his arm was around her waist. "I thought you were sleeping late today," he said chidingly.

"Every intention; but there's something about the sound of the ocean; it can pry you out of the warmest bed." She nipped a kiss into his neck, pleased with the salt taste of his red-brown skin. In a week's time he had tanned marvelously, while she had been forced to sit on the porch in the shade, recovering from the folly of her initial day in the sun. He was also filling out, she noticed with satisfaction. There seemed to be some padding over his ribs. She pinched to make sure. He rubbed fish odor into her hair and she ducked away hastily, began uncovering their breakfast. There was a plate of fresh tropical fruit—papaya, melon, pineapple—two platters of ham and eggs, a large basket filled with muffins. And one little plate had two letters on it.

"Mail," she said, and sliced the envelopes open with a butter knife. She was reading when Doremus came back from washing up. He bent over nonchalantly to kiss a bare and somewhat flaky arm.

"Who's that one from?"

"Helen," she said.

He yawned, cracked his jaws, poured another cup of coffee.

"How's everything back in The Shades?"

"Normal," Amy said, absorbed in the letter. As she was reading, a wisp of shadow crossed her face. She put the letter down beside her plate and stared off toward the water. A man on horseback came along the beach, disappeared down the line of cottages.

"Something?" he said, after a while.

"Oh . . . no, it's all right." But she left the table and stood with her back to him.

"Peggy's all right, I hope."

"Yes, fine. They're all fine. They had a picnic the other day. The three of them—Helen, Peg and Peter. Helen says Peter is talking quite a lot now, when he forgets himself. That's usually when he's around Peg. When they're together they're in their own little world." Amy's head dropped slightly.

"And we're . . . in our own little world, and I've never been happier, so why can't I forget about it, all of it? Am I going to be haunted the rest of my life, am I always going to get the shakes when I think of . . . Craig?"

Doremus put his napkin down thoughtfully, got up, guided her to the ornamental couch. "No, you aren't," he said. "Keep in mind that it's only been five months. Some kinds of shock don't wear off in a hurry. What you went through was the equivalent of a particularly nasty combat operation. There are men alive today still having nightmares about World War Two. Give yourself a little time, Amy. In our little world."

She nodded, but she was still tense. He put an arm around her, which brought a smile. She leaned gratefully against him. "I have the peculiar feeling that I was supposed to die. Sometimes at night I'm absolutely sure that I don't deserve . . . this life, that I don't deserve you. I'm absolutely convinced it's all going to be snatched away after a short trial period."

"Try to get you away from me," he said.

"I love you so very much, Doremus. I don't think you're ever off my mind. When you're out there in the dark fishing I get a little scared. Now it's fine. Now I feel even a little bit brave and confident. But I don't like for you to go away even for an hour. I'm talking like a—"

"A wife," he said. "What happened to the appetite?"

She looked at him sheepishly. "I've got a stupid question, as long as I'm in this mood. Then I'll shut up forever. Doremus . . . what made you pick me? I was sure you were in love with Helen. I thought I recognized all the symptoms. I had made

249

up my mind. Amy's Blue Period. You were going to marry Helen. I was going to join the Salvation Army or something. Then, out of nowhere that afternoon, 'I think it's time to get married, Amy.' "

"Very romantic of me," he said, his lip curling. "As long as we're opening up, let me say I was scared stiff. I thought I was too old for you. I expected withering scorn."

"Anything but a blubbery face and a very delighted girl in your lap. Too old! When you're a hundred and nineteen I'll be a hundred and one. But you didn't tell me yet. Helen is a damned good-looking, mature and thoughtful woman. She has style and serenity. What did you want with me? It wasn't sympathy, was it?"

"Sure."

"Oh, thanks a lot!"

"I was feeling sorry for myself. Tossing in bed at night like a sixteen-year-old virgin. Fumbling around. Not eating right. I was very sorry for myself because you were on my mind, Amy. As you are now, as you always will be. And Helen wasn't."

She looked closely at his face, then nodded. "That simple, hey?"

"That's all there is to it. I loved Amy Lawlor and I'm glad I was man enough to tell her. Now I'm hungry enough to eat two breakfasts instead of one if you don't get over to the table before I do. And then I think when I'm chock full I'll wander down to the hotel and send a cable to Nelson in Chicago telling him that it'll be my pleasure to represent his fine detective agency in the city of San Francisco and to wire me a couple of thousand dollars care of Barclay's because I'm on my honeymoon and I want to treat my bride to a trunkful of new clothes. And then I think we ought to get in that little Ford out there and—"

"Whoa, whoa," Amy said quickly, kissing him. He held her very tightly and for quite a long time, and one of the tall hotel waiters walking by turned his head at such an angle he almost lost the tray he was toting.

"On second thought," Doremus said with a vague smile, "I think I'll forget about the breakfast for now, and I can always send the wire this afternoon. Or some other time."

"Or some other time," Amy repeated, and obediently followed him into the shady cottage.

BESTSELLING TERROR
BY JOHN FARRIS

☐ ☐	51082-8	ALL HEADS TURN WHEN THE HUNT GOES BY	$3.95 Canada $4.95
☐ ☐	50008-3 50009-1	THE AXMAN COMETH	$4.50 Canada $5.50
☐ ☐	51782-2 51783-0	THE CAPTORS	$3.95 Canada $4.95
☐	51786-5	FIENDS	$4.95 Canada $5.95
☐ ☐	51784-9 51785-7	THE FURY	$3.95 Canada $4.95
☐ ☐	51793-8	KING WINDOM	$4.95 Canada $5.95
☐ ☐	58258-6 58259-4	MINOTAUR	$3.95 Canada $4.95
☐ ☐	50300-7 50299-X	SCARE TACTICS	$4.95 Canada $5.95
☐ ☐	51788-1 51789-X	SHARP PRACTICE	$3.95 Canada $4.95
☐ ☐	58266-7 58267-5	SON OF THE ENDLESS NIGHT	$4.50 Canada $5.50
☐ ☐	58270-5 58271-3	WILDWOOD	$4.50 Canada $5.95

Buy them at your local bookstore or use this handy coupon:
Clip and mail this page with your order.

Publishers Book and Audio Mailing Service
P.O. Box 120159, Staten Island, NY 10312-0004

Please send me the book(s) I have checked above. I am enclosing $ _____
(Please add $1.25 for the first book, and $.25 for each additional book to cover postage and handling.
Send check or money order only—no CODs.)

Name _____

Address _____

City _____ State/Zip _____

Please allow six weeks for delivery. Prices subject to change without notice.